Diamante Publications Presents

Touch A

Woman's Soul

Inked by KS Oliver

Dedication from K.S. Oliver

I dedicate this book and every other that I ink to my husband B. Abby.

You are more than just the love of my life but my friend and my biggest supporter.

To my children (KS) Kwan & Shaun. We did it again.

I can't thank the two of you enough for teaching me every day about what it is to truly love unconditionally. Thank you for picking me of all people to be your mom.

I am truly blessed.

To my brothers Ajmal Acklin, and Jarvis Jones (S.I.P)

To my brother Khayree Y. Acklin I had the pleasure of being involved in 19 years of your life before you were taken away. I can't believe that I won't get that call from you today saying hey sis your book dropped yet? That's ok I know I am making you proud of me. My birthday will never be the same but I promise to keep reaching towards the top just like you would have wanted me to.

KS Oliver

Acknowledgements from KS Oliver

I want to first thank God for keeping me and Blessing me with the ability to write a story. I've been through it all and some, but it has only humbled me and made me even stronger. I am made of bricks now.

To my parents (Clarine & C.O) and my grandparents (Mary & Woody Oliver), my mother in law Rose Abby, my sister in law Claudette Davis, my step dad Leroy White and my step mom Desiree Thornton- Oliver. Thank you for everything. You have supported me in everything I have set out to do. I appreciate each of you and the unique things that you bring out of me.

Thank you to my A1's LeTorri Mitchell, Latrice Burns, Marissa Palmer, Nadia Brown, Karen Cabret, Natasha Hill, Angel Taylor, and Tara Waters. Each of you bring something different to my life and I appreciate you for it.

KS Oliver

S/O to the Literary Ladies of the ATL. Thank you for always being there when I needed you and when I didn't.

Sunny Giovanni man we have laughed, fought and cried. I appreciate you and all of your hard work.

Thank you to all of my readers. Special S/O to Janata McDaniel, Andreas McMurtry, , Melanie Moses, Priscilla Murray, Audrey Hargraves, Priscilla Murray, Angelina Butler, Denise Gilliam, Stacy Leonard, Ebonee Dunbar, Tamara Williams, Shana "Mousey" Hargrave, Shamika Payne, Rosezenia Cummings, Sherry Boose, and Mama Jane Panella. I couldn't do this without y'all. Each of you have supported me and provided so much encouragement. I so appreciate you.

Diamonds are forever and so is my team. Shout out to Diamante' Publications, thanks to all of you for the constant support.

Ashley Antoinette that talk meant everything to me and I want you to know I heard every word. Thank you...

KS Oliver

Last but not least my mini me and codefendant

Vette, we do this. I am so proud of you and all your hard

work.

Prologue

How it all started...

Mendosa's presence always commanded all the attention in the room. That was the reason Amore was smitten. After all, she was only twenty years old when she laid eyes on him. At an impressionable age, she didn't have that much experience with men like the one in front of her.

"Hey, I'm Mendosa. What's your name, beautiful? Do you take voyages often?" His accent was already a show stopper, but as an unexpected gesture, he kissed her hand and then exposed that engaging smile of his.

"Amore, and no, not really," she simply said as she blushed and looked at the paintings displayed on the wall of the vintage shop. She and her roommate Kiana were spending their spring break in Panama. She wanted to buy a keepsake to put on her bedroom wall to commemorate her trip. It was Amore's very first time outside of the US. Her caramel toned skin with red undertones showed that the sexy stranger was getting to her, and he was hardly even trying.

With shy, dark brown eyes hidden behind long lashes, high cheekbones, full lips, and shoulder length, loose curls that framed her face, Mendosa was quickly taken by her innocence. Most women that he met gave off the impression of being a little too easy.

His skin was the color of toasted almonds and his soft, light brown eyes seemed familiar. As his white teeth glistened, Amore could feel her body weaken. She was enamored by the good-looking young man. He was 6'6, and his body was muscular and solid. Lacking a father figure all her life, she had a knack for falling in love with the opposite sex a little too fast. She promised herself that she would take her time and get to know a man first before getting her heart involved. Even more pressing was making sure she didn't end up in bed with him too soon. Often, she'd messed up by giving her body up way too quickly.

She'd lost her virginity when she was sixteen to a no-good neighborhood hustler by the name of Cameron, and that was all she'd written. He'd shattered her heart into a million pieces by cheating on her with a girl in her class named, Caprice, so from that day forward, she vowed to be more cautious. She didn't want to end up like her mother; a shell of the woman she once was because of a man. Being the product of an extra-marital affair, Amore knew what it felt like to be unwanted by her own daddy. There was no way she was going to repeat history as a grown woman. She was determined to make sure her children had a mother and father to show them what true love really was. She also refused to love a man who didn't return that love.

"It's nice to meet you, Amore. You are so gorgeous." His smoldering eyes stayed on hers. She later learned that Mendosa was originally from Panama but lived in Miami, Florida. He just happened to be visiting too. Well, she later learned that he was sneaking in and out.

Mendosa was the sole provider for his parents' household, because of their low wages. His mother was a maid, and his father was a landscaper. The money he made off the drug trade tended to cover more than his parents' income did. They eventually stopped trying to sway him from the streets, causing him to drop out of high school to divulge fully in that lifestyle.

When the authorities came knocking on their door with an arrest warrant for seventeen- year old Mendosa, he and his parents were in route to Miami, Florida for a new start. He promised them that he would get his GED and take up a trade. The hustler in him was still there, so that promise went out of the door as soon as he stepped foot in the US.

Like a magnet to trouble, Mendosa seemed to attract unsavory characters into his life. Red, a gang leader and drug kingpin noticed the young man's swag off top. In no time, Mendosa was doing exactly what he and his parents had run from before. This time, he knew to keep a low profile.

When he met Amore, he'd surpassed Red in the drug game. Red was getting high on his own supply, so he fell off the wagon fast. It was Mendosa's time, and he took over a market that was wide open. However, he was frivolous with his money. His preoccupation was money, clothes, and cars. Investing and having assets were notions that he was unfamiliar with. That was until he met the love of his life. That was when things changed for the better. What Amore and Mendosa didn't know was, there were those lurking and waiting to take what they'd worked so hard and diligently for.

Amore had managed to scrape up the money for that trip to Panama by working at a deli not far from Spelman College where she was studying for her degree in Business. So far, her grade point average was a 4.0 because she'd managed to avoid distractions such as Mendosa's fine ass. Still, there was something about the obviously streetwise man in front of her that left her intrigued. They ended up exchanging numbers and after some months had passed, their relationship blossomed into something official.

After a year or so of courtship, the two were married by a judge at the Fulton County courthouse with no reception or celebration afterward. All the young lovers wanted was a secure, stable relationship and plenty of babies. Mendosa ended up moving to Atlanta, but his drug empire in Miami continued to flourish.

"I want at least ten kids. Five sons and five daughters," Mendosa had told her as they lay on their marital bed in an empty one-bedroom apartment in Atlanta's affluent Buckhead neighborhood.

*   *   *

After six years of trying, Mendosa and Amore were about ready to give up on being parents. She's suffered from years of endometriosis and had a tilted uterus. Carrying a baby full-term seemed next to impossible even if she did get pregnant.

"I'm so sorry Mr. and Mrs. Saldana. The massive scar tissue blocking Mrs. Saldana's fallopian tubes may be making it hard for you to conceive. Also, it seems that your eggs are viable, Mrs. Saldana, but your husband's sperm just can't seem to make it fertilize them. There are options. We can use viable eggs and sperm from you both and implant them in a surrogate, or we can try to implant them in you, Mrs. Saldana. The only thing with that is the risk of you having to be on bed rest most of your pregnancy."

Wiping tears from her weary eyes, Amore spoke up. "I'd love to carry my own baby. We'll do whatever it takes for me to be able to give birth."

Mendosa held on to his wife's hand and nodded in adamant agreement. "Surrogacy will be the last option, doctor. Are you sure I'm not the issue?"

Doctor Kozier nodded. "No, you're not, Mr. Saldana. Your sperm count is rather substantial. We may have more viable sperm than eggs. However, we can try a round of In Vitro Fertilization. I have to warn you that it's very costly."

"We don't care about the cost." Mendosa squeezed his wife's hand and stared anxiously at the doctor.

"Okay, we can get started as soon as possible."

"If that's what you want honey." Mendosa's eyes held Amore's.

Amore looked up at her spouse lovingly. "That's definitely what I want."

It actually took two rounds of In Vitro Fertilization before anything happened. Soon, Vintage Amore Saldana was born. She was the love of her mother's life, thus explaining her middle name.

A little over two years later, Amore woke up to excruciating abdominal pain. Being a work out fanatic, she was obsessed with getting her pre-baby body back. With normal periods and no signs of pregnancy, Sage, their second born, came unexpectantly with no In Vitro. Miracle was her middle name. Mendosa and Amore did not expect her arrival, because they thought getting pregnant naturally was impossible. Yet, they loved their second born equally as much as their first.

Years passed and their family, as well as finances, were flourishing. Mendosa was hell-bent on taking on a legal lifestyle. He didn't have the sons he'd wanted, but his daughters were just as vital to keeping his namesake going. He decided to invest in legal businesses for their stability. Hence, MS Real Estate was born. The company started out small, but it thrived due to money from private investors and Mendosa's drug money.

When Vintage was eighteen and Sage was fifteen, everything shifted. The two young ladies were spending a couple weeks with their grandparents in Miami for summer vacation before discovering their parents' bodies when they returned home. They had been murdered execution style while they slept in their bed. It appeared to be a home invasion style robbery. Jewelry and a safe full of money had been taken. That left Vintage and Sage parentless, but they'd been left a substantial amount of money in life insurance and assets. What they didn't know was, they were rich, vulnerable targets for many faceless, nameless vultures.

Chapter 1

"Oh my, this dress is gorgeous!" The tall, blonde-haired white woman held one of the store's couture gowns up to her body as she stared in the mirror in longing.

"It's one of my favorites," Vintage smiled pleasantly, making her way over to her customer.

"How much?"

Because the items in the boutique were so expensive, they didn't have price tags on them. She'd chosen a cream and bronze embezzled gown with a low cut, corset top. The bottom flared out but had a thigh-high split on the left side to add some sexiness. "Seven hundred dollars."

"Oh, wow, that's a steal. Your store is amazing might I add. I must try this on. I have an event next weekend, and this will be perfect. I'm all late finding a gown, but I came across your boutique online."

"I'm happy to know that the new ad is actually
gaining some traction. Thank you. Sure, follow me, so
you can try it on."

A few minutes later she walked out of the dressing
room looking fabulous. "Wow," Vintage's eyes widened.
That is definitely the one." She looked great, and Vintage
was trying to get that sale. Normally, she didn't work in
the store, but the sales-associate who'd been scheduled
had fallen ill. That meant that she had to cover for a few
hours until another sales-associate could get there on
such short notice.

"You think?" the woman quizzed before doing a twirl
in front of the mirrors that aligned the wall.

"Think? You can see yourself."

Beaming, she looked back at Vintage. "You're right.
I'm getting this gown." With a giddy smile on her face,
she went back in the dressing room to change into her
clothes.

Vintage couldn't help but stare at herself in the
mirror. With a dark brown complexion, she dripped

flawless melanin. One thing that she loved was her smooth skin. With sensual, dark brown eyes with long lashes, an angular nose and full lips, she was attractive by most standards. Her curvy figure and round black girl booty were gifts from her beautiful mother. Standing at 5'6 and weighing a hundred forty pounds, Vintage embraced who stared back at her.

In no time, the woman came out of the dressing room, interrupting her thoughts. Soon, the transaction was done, and she left satisfied.

Vintage's sister Sage ran the online store and was in charge of marketing the boutique as well. The big dream was to open a chain of stores all over the world, not just the US. Sage was younger than Vintage. At nineteen years old, she was more into that social media stuff. Constantly on Instagram and Facebook, Sage had a plethora of followers and friends. That was a plus for Vintage, being that she wasn't into social media like that. She'd use it as necessary, but Sage had more of a niche for promoting the boutique's merchandise that way.

Often, she'd set up photo-shoots and have models showcase the boutique's fashions. That brought on a lot of sales. The next thing on the agenda was to make sure the online Fall catalog was complete by the end of the month.

Their mother had opened the store years ago. Once her daughters were older, she felt the need to do something with herself. One thing she loved was shopping and looking good. Besides, Mendosa had his "business" and spent a lot of time away. Vintage figured her mother wanted her own identity in some way, so Mi Amore Vintage Boutique was born.

The interest that Vintage and Sage had shown in the business when it was handed down to them made it flourish and become even more profitable after their mother's death. A comforting thought to Vintage was that she was looking down on them in pride.

The bell on the door chimed, alerting her that someone had just walked in. When she looked up, she saw Kellie and was so relieved. Not that she didn't enjoy working in the boutique, but she had to leave asap.

"Kellie, thank God you're here." She was a good friend of Sage's and the assistant manager, so Vintage trusted her to hold it down. "Melissa will be here in a couple hours."

With a nod, she put her Starbucks coffee cup on the counter. "I got this. You go ahead and handle your business."

Glancing down at her rose gold and diamond encrusted Lady Rolex, Vintage headed toward the door. Her classic, black Red Bottoms clicked loudly on the black and gray Italian marble floor.

"Right, thanks again. I know you were supposed to be off today."

"It's fine. That commission check's going to look good. No complaints over here." Kellie waved at her and grinned slyly.

With a laugh, they exchanged goodbyes before Vintage made her way to her silver Beemer. As she pulled off, she coasted her way into the early afternoon traffic. Reaching in her purse, she pulled out her cell and made a call.

After two rings, a man answered. "I'm already here waiting. Shit, I got other shit to do, Vintage."

"I'll be there in thirty minutes…"

"Thirty minutes. That's too long," he hissed. "You told me you'd be here when I got here."

"I planned to, but I had to go into the shop today. Look, just… just wait until I get there. Hopefully, traffic won't be too bad, and I'll get there sooner."

"Either that or…"

"Or what, Joshua? You're going to break into my house and get your things?" With a slight chuckle, Vintage pretended not to be bothered by her ex. They'd been together for almost two years, and slowly but surely, he'd moved his stuff into her house. Then he moved in without talking it over with her. At first, she let it go, because she was really feeling him. That all came to a screeching halt when he realized that she wasn't planning to have sex with him right away. At the age of twenty-two, she was proudly still a virgin.

One thing Amore had done was tell her daughters about the reality of sex. Vintage was eighteen when her parents were murdered, but her mom had taught her some valuable lessons about her worth as a woman.

"I had given up my virginity way too soon to the wrong man. After that, I didn't seem to care as much. It was like once my worth had been compromised, I didn't have the will to claim it back. After I met your father, it was slowly replenished. I don't want you to give away your self-worth. If you feel that you love a man, don't rush. If he loves you, he'll wait. I'm not saying wait until your wedding night, but at least wait until you know he's at least considering marrying you." She'd told Vintage that when she was sixteen.

Her sister Sage didn't take their mother's lessons to heart like she did. She'd lost her virginity when she was fifteen and hadn't stopped since. A junior at Spelman College, she'd graduated from high school when she was sixteen. Her major was Business, and she was maintaining a 4.0 GPA. With her education and business skills in order, she didn't have the same focus when it came to the opposite sex. Sage would often hop from one man to the next and was a self-proclaimed player. Vintage laughed out loud at the differences between herself and her sister. In four years, Sage had bedded more men than Vintage would in a lifetime. That was her life though, and Vintage didn't judge her.

Joshua's black Range Rover was in the driveway when Vintage pulled up. Making sure not to park behind him, so he could leave right after he got his things, she didn't want to have yet another confrontation with that man. She'd told him early in the relationship that she wanted to wait until her wedding night to lose her virginity. Of course, he only went along with it because he thought she'd relent and give it up. His game wasn't that damn tight.

"You really think I'm going to keep lying beside you every night with a hard dick? It's plenty of women out there who'll give it up!" He'd snapped on her the night she decided to call it quits.

After finding out about his cheating ways, because she had cracked the code on his cell phone, she kicked him out. "I'll be back to get my things later!" That was his way of prolonging the break up a few weeks ago. The day before, Vintage realized how tired she was of seeing his clothes in her closet and his toiletries in her bathroom. He was a pro-gamer who made six figures a year simply playing video games. He'd left his PlayStation 4 there with a lot of his games.

"Either you come to get your stuff tomorrow, or I'm throwing it out," she'd threatened after calling him.

Josh let out an exasperated breath. "Alright. What time?"

"One pm works for me, and it should work for you too being that you don't have a job to go to."

"I work from home," he threw in. "Don't knock my hustle."

"I'm not. Just be here at one."

After that, Vintage hung up and the next morning got the call that she had to open the boutique. That threw the plan off and hopefully

Josh would just get his things and be on his way. She didn't have the time for his attitude. When she first met him, he seemed to be so calm and even-tempered. Eventually, his true colors came out and he was argumentative and confrontational. Not one for drama or chaos, Vintage knew that it was best to leave him alone.

"Finally." Joshua slammed the door of his SUV before walking ahead of her.

Taking her time, Vintage knew that his impatience was what really had him all uptight. He had time to play video games all day though. It was obvious that people made time for what they wanted to do. That was fine by her because she was done. Maybe if he'd deserved it, she may have changed her mind about waiting for marriage to give her virginity to him. Knowing that he was out there giving it up to any chick who wanted it, she wasn't willing to risk what could possibly come with giving up what she held so dear. What would be the pay-out for her sacrifice? Nothing but heartache and pain, she was sure.

"I have somewhere to be in the next couple hours, so hurry up please," Vintage threw over her shoulder as she walked past him.

"Oh, so now you wanna rush me?" The way his slanted, light brown eyes were brewing with anger told her not to push his buttons any further.

"I'm just saying get to it. It's no point in rubbing in the fact that I wasn't here when you got here. I'm here now so get your things and leave please."

"Okay." He shrugged. "Whatever."

As he went off to get his belongings, Vintage kicked her heels off and headed toward her favorite recliner in the sitting room. Massaging her aching temples, she wondered if she'd ever had a moment of peace in her life. At a young age, she had an old soul and only longed to find that one true love.

Less than thirty minutes later, Josh returned to the first floor with his suitcase and PlayStation in hand. "Have you seen my black and gray Burberry shirt?"

"No," I simply stated as I stood. "Whatever you left here was in the closet. Maybe you took it with you."

"I didn't. It's here somewhere."

"And if it is, I'll find it and ship it to you. Just give me your new address."

"Oh, so it's like that now? I can't come to get it if you find it?" His handsome, caramel-toned face was all balled up in a scowl as he asked.

"Why would you even want to? It's over between us, and I damn sure can't do anything else with the shirt. Besides, you probably took it to the cleaner's or something." Puzzled as to why he was so adamant about coming over to get a shirt, it occurred to her. He wasn't ready to let her go that easily, but his pride was in the way, and the shirt was just an excuse to come back.

"It's all good, Vin. If you find the shirt ship it to me." Shaking his head, he made his way to the door.

"Why have an attitude about it? This isn't even about a shirt, is it? I told you that I wanted to make sure I'm with the right man before I have sex, and you said you respected that. As a matter of fact, you said you admired that..."

"That's when you were nineteen. I thought you'd give up on that little girl fantasy and be a real damn woman, but you didn't. I'm a man, and I need to have sex. I love you, but I sleep with other women. If only you could've accepted that and gone with the flow, we would've eventually gotten married. Maybe if I was getting some, I could've been faithful."

"Wow, you're really an asshole." Opening the door, Vintage tried her best not to yell at him. "Leave now, please and thank you."

"Fine, but I hope you know that no man our age is going to wait for you. You're in a fairytale land, little girl." As he smirked at her, he crossed the door's threshold.

Slamming it behind him, Vintage locked it hoping she'd never see Josh's face again in life. As she headed up the stairs to get ready for a fundraiser for sickle-cell, her phone rang.

"Sage, what's going on?" Her mood had changed in an instant. Well, at least she pretended it had, so her sister wouldn't be nosey.

"Hey, Vin. I'm at the convention center now unloading the dresses for the auction. When will you be here?" she asked.

"Oh, yeah. Uh, give me about an hour. I'm about to get dressed."

"Okay, but don't be late. I need you to help me set up."

"I thought you had Danielle there to help you."

"Uh, when did I tell you that?"

Vintage's head had been in the clouds lately. "You told me that weeks ago." Was she wrong?

"No, I told you that Danielle was going to help me find some girls for the catalog. Are you okay, sis? You seem really... different lately."

"I'm fine. Just a misunderstanding. I'll see you in a few."

Ending the call, Vintage wondered why she'd been so discombobulated lately. There was so much on her mind and the stress of it was taking a toll. Lately, she'd been really missing her parents, and it wasn't easy that she and her sister had once been suspects in their murders. The crime was still unsolved, and she often wondered if their murderer would ever be caught.

Chapter 2

Not even an hour after they'd discovered their
parents' bodies four years ago, Sage and Vintage were
hauled off to the police station for questioning. To Sage,
it was more like an interrogation. They treated them as if
they were two little spoiled, rich, black girls who didn't
deserve the privilege they'd been afforded.

That was probably due to the fact that they suspected
that their father ran a drug empire, but he was so good at
finessing the system they couldn't prove it. Therefore,
they treated Sage and Vintage as if they were the
criminals to punish a dead man.

"So, which one of your little boyfriends did you get to
execute your parents?" Detective Adams, a middle-aged
white man with a receding hairline asked.

"You can't be serious," Sage told him. She was way
beyond her fifteen years. "I just lost both of my parents
and you accuse me of murdering them?" Shaking her

head, she continued after swallowing the lump in her throat. The tears flowed down her face anyway. "Find whoever did this, because you're wasting your time questioning me!"

In another room, Vintage was being questioned by a younger black detective. He was tall, and a little stout with a protruding belly in his tight, white button down. "Calm down, young lady. I'm sure there's a life insurance policy on your folks and you and your sister are beneficiaries. Did your mama beat you? Did she mentally abuse you? Did you father molest you? What's the motive behind this crime?" Detective Warren asked as he rubbed his hands together in hopes of a confession of some kind.

"First of all, my sister and I were out of town when this happened. Secondly, no, my parents didn't do anything to us but be good parents, believe it or not. As far as a life insurance policy, I don't know anything about that, nor do I care. I love my mother and father, and there's no way I'd ever hurt them for any reason. You're reaching, sir."

The detective looked like he was offended, but he had no reason at all to be. Vintage was just stating facts. No amount of money would ever equate to her parents' lives. All she wanted to do was grieve, but instead, she was fighting for her freedom.

"We don't have anything against you now, but..."

The door busted open and it was Sage and Vintage's grandparents.

"Why are you questioning them without us or a lawyer present? Sage is a minor!" Grandma Rosa said sternly.

Grandma Rosa and Grandpa Nick were both being questioned at the house when an officer whisked Vintage and Sage off to the station.

Grandpa Nick spoke up next. "And it's obvious that you think they are suspects, which is absurd. Those girls have been with us in Miami the entire summer. It's no way they're involved. Even if they had been here, there's no way. They love their mother and father. Now, you release them into our custody, or you will have a lawsuit on your ass."

The detective was prepared to contest the fact that the two girls were parentless, and guardianship hadn't been given to them. Grandma Rosa was ready with a document in her hand that proved that in the event that anything happened to them, Sage and Vintage would legally be released into their custody.

They took them back to their home after that. Soon, they relocated to Atlanta after selling their house in Miami to be closer to their granddaughters. The years flew by and there weren't any more suspects. With no witnesses and no physical evidence, the case went cold.

*   *   *

Sage woke up the morning after the fundraiser benefit gala with a lot on her mind. It was Monday morning, and her first class wasn't until one pm. She'd set it up that way on purpose because studious or not, she loved to enjoy life. Not wanting to set herself up to miss a class so close to receiving her BS, she made sure she had ample time to get up and make it to campus after a long weekend of partying. Sage's intelligence seemed to be natural, so she didn't really need to study much

That morning she had an early session with Bryan, a student that she tutored in Calculus. Normally they'd meet up later in the evening, but he needed an hour session to prepare for a big test that would count towards twenty-five percent of his grade.

After a light breakfast of toast, scrambled eggs, and turkey bacon, she was dressed in a pair of sweatpants and a tank-top. There was no need to be all professional. It wasn't like she was his professor or something. The sound of her condo's doorbell rang, and she made her way over to let Bryan in.

He was fine as hell, standing at six feet even with almond toned skin, wavy hair and sexy dark brown eyes. The deep dimples in his cheeks and high cheekbones along with all those muscles made her forget that he was the same age she was. Normally, she went for older men, but Bryan was an exception. As she reached to close the door behind her, Bryan pulled her into his hard body.

"Damn, I missed you," he told her breathlessly before pulling her tank top over her head.

Sage allowed him to take one of her hardened nipples into his warm, wet mouth before letting out a low moan. "Mmm, we only have an hour…"

"All I need is ten minutes. All I wanna do is taste you. I'll feel you later."

Not one to refuse a good head session, Sage allowed him to pull her sweats off and carry her over to the sofa. Once she was seated, he got down on his knees and ducked between her thighs. The way he teased her sensitivity made her shudder in pleasure as she held on to the back of his head. Staring down at him, she bit down on her bottom lip as he licked and sucked on her hardened clitoris.

"Ohh… mmm… Bryan… ohhh…" Her eyes closed, and she slid down to the end of the sofa's cushion, spreading her thighs wider. "Damn…" she whispered, losing control of her own body as it overheated and trembled.

"You taste so sweet... mmm..."

Sage wondered how a nineteen-year-old could be so skilled with his tongue. His thick lips were wet and glistening with her juices as his eyes caught hers.

"Bryan... I'm... I'm... mmm." Not able to get the words out, she let the orgasm take over her senses. Her legs shook, and her knees weakened as a warm sensation traveled from her fingertips to her toes.

Licking his lips, Bryan stood to his feet and then sat down beside Sage. With that feeling of euphoria still coursing through her veins, she couldn't move. The thing was, she wanted more than that. Bryan was working with something and when her strength returned seconds later, she grabbed the bulge in his pants. "Uh, you started this. You know that, right?"

He chuckled. "You're something else."

"But you like it though," she countered in a sultry voice.

"Mmm... I love it," he admitted as she straddled him.

Unbuckling his belt, she unbuttoned and then unzipped his pants before helping him push them down to his ankles. As she leaned over, she opened a drawer and retrieved a condom. Sage was always ready and had condoms in drawers all over her place.

Lowering her wetness onto his shaft, she closed her eyes knowing that she was way too addicted to that part of a man's anatomy. Sadly, her feelings for them stopped there. For some reason, her heart and mind didn't join her body in the ecstasy. It was all physical, and unfortunately sometimes the men she partook in pleasure with caught feelings. Not able to return them, she didn't care when they gave up and moved on. She only cared when they didn't and started acting obsessed. It had happened a couple times before. So far, Bryan seemed cool with their little arrangement, but how long would that last?

* * *

Sage's last class of the day ended at four and she headed to her champagne colored Benz in a hurry. All she wanted to do was lounge and smoke a blunt or something. It had already been a long day, and she was ready for it to end. The only thing was, she had to work on the boutique's catalog.

"I'm on the way home," she told Danielle after speed dialing her number.

"Okay boo, I'm on my way. I got some shots you need to look over." Danielle was Sage's best friend and a professional photographer.

"See you in a few. Bring a bottle of something, girl." Sage knew she wasn't old enough to drink, but that didn't stop her. She was about to turn twenty in about three months and Danielle had just turned twenty-one a week before.

"What do you want?" Danielle knew that her friend was picky about everything, and if she showed up with just any kind of liquor, Sage would just turn her snooty ass nose up.

"Get some Patron or something," Sage suggested.

"Okay, I'll be there in a little while."

Ending the call, Sage noticed that she had a text from Bryan.

Bryan: WYD

She hated that wyd mess and decided to ignore him. Thankfully, when she pulled up to her place, Danielle wasn't there yet. Unlocking her door after taking the elevator to the third floor, she noticed that her phone was ringing in her black Tory Burch tote bag. Trying to grab it as she closed the door behind her, she didn't get to it before it stopped ringing. She looked down at the screen and noticed that it was Vintage who'd been calling. She called her back once she was comfy in a pair of black BeBe lounge pants and a black t-shirt.

"Hey, Miss Eligible Bachelorette. All the men in the place were on you last night," Sage joked with her sister glad that she was done with Joshua's obnoxious ass. He'd come on to her many times before, but Sage kept it to herself knowing that her sister would see right through that dog in due time.

"What are you talking about?" Vintage asked although she knew what her sister was referring to. One tall, handsome dark-skinned cup of hot chocolate had insisted on dancing with Vintage most of the night, and Sage hadn't had a chance to ask about him.

"You know who and what I'm talking about. Who is he and are you going to go out with him or what? He was fine, Vin. You know you lost feelings for Josh a long time ago. It's time to move on and..."

"Move on with a stranger? Lil' sis, you have no shame." Vintage laughed, but Sage didn't.

"And why should I? Men play the field all the time. Josh had no problem moving on, so why the hell shouldn't you?"

"It's not about him, and you know that, Sage. It's well, you know how I am about getting attached. Ever since we lost mom and dad, I feel better keeping those I love at a minimum."

"You're only twenty-two years old, Vin. You don't have to be in love to date. Just don't get your feelings involved. That's your problem. You have to take it for what it is. Enjoy life. You only have one. If anything, you should know that."

Vintage sighed. "I do, but you know me. I want the husband and kids one day. I don't have it in me to just... go out with random men."

"How can you get the husband and kids if you don't take a chance? Tell me you at least gave that fine ass man your number. If not, you're really missing out. He was dressed to kill too. Mmm, couldn't have been me."

"I know," Vintage said with a chuckle.

"Forget you," Sage couldn't help but laugh.

The sound of the doorbell made her put an end to their call. "Sis, that's Danie. I'm going to call you back later."

"Y'all better be working on that catalog."

"We are, boss," Sage joked and pressed the END button.

Opening the door for Danielle, she led her friend straight to the kitchen to make their drinks.

"Don't you think we should drink after we work?" Danielle asked.

"No, and stop being a goody-goody." Sage rolled her eyes before pulling two glasses from the cabinet.

After filling them with ice, liquor and pineapple juice, she told Danielle to follow her to her office. Vintage still lived in their parents' estate, but Sage had opted to spend some of her inheritance on a condo. Their home just had too many memories that she chose not to deal with, so her own little space was needed.

"Before we get to business, I got some tea," Danielle took a huge gulp of her drink before putting her glass on a coaster on the end table.

"What? Not Miss Good Girl. You don't even make tea," Sage teased with a sly grin on her face.

"Oh hush, everybody's not like you. Listen though, girl."

Sage wiped the smile off her face. "Okay, I'm all ears."

"So, you know I've been dating Quentin, right?"

"Um, yeah." Quentin Jones was a pro-football player for the Falcons and she'd been hired to do a private photo-shoot for him. That was how they had met three months ago.

"Of course, get to the point, boo, damn. We don't have all night."

Shaking her head, Danielle laughed. "Well, he told me that he wants to take things to the next level and make our relationship official." She held her hand out showing the bling I'd managed to miss.

"What? Okay, good for you, but that's the tea? Are y'all engaged?" Happy for her friend, Sage was disappointed that her tea wasn't so hot.

"No, not yet. It's just a token." She took in a deep breath and continued. "His ex-girlfriend is the problem. She ended up showing up at the restaurant where we were having dinner last night. How she knew we were there, I have no clue. He says she must've followed us. Either way, she was watching us the entire time, so we decided to leave. That heifer was already outside and had the nerve to try to jump on me. Quentin made sure we didn't fight, but I don't know if I want to go there with him with all that drama going on."

"Girl, bye. Not only is Quentin a good-looking man, but he got bank. You better secure that bag and stop talking crazy. That chick is a non-issue. As long as she doesn't put her hands on you, you're good. If she does, take out a warrant. It's that simple. Eventually, she'll move on and dig the gold out of another sucker's pockets."

"You think so?" Danielle's frown made Sage feel like she may be giving her friend the wrong advice, but what the hell. Quentin was a millionaire, so there was no point in her letting the next chick have him. He was a catch. "I don't be fighting over no dude," Danielle added.

"Who said fight over him? You don't have to fight that chick. Just do what I said, Danie. You'll think me later, and don't sign no prenup either."

"You know you're silly. We ain't even been an official couple for two days." Danielle pulled her MacBook out of the carrying case. "Let me show you these pictures before I get too damn drunk to function."

"Yeah, because I have to send the last shots to the graphic designer by noon tomorrow." Sage leaned forward, so she would have a good view of the computer screen.

Suddenly there was a loud knock at the door. Whoever it was hadn't even bothered to ring the doorbell, so it made Sage think the visit was personal. "What the?" she pondered, sauntering over to the front door.

When she saw that it was Bryan, she let out a frustrated sigh. He knew not to just pop up at her place without talking to her first. Swinging the door open, her attitude was on ten. Bryan glared at her with a pissed look on his face.

"Why ain't you been answering my damn calls?" he asked.

There was no way that she was inviting him in or entertaining the conversation at that point. He was on one, and she didn't have time for it. "You need to leave, Bryan because you're obviously in your feelings for nothing. I'm busy and you know better than coming over here unannounced."

"You got some nigga in here?" Attempting to look over her shoulder, he closed the distance between them.

Sage pushed him back. "What the hell are you doing? Whom I have over here is none of your business, Quent."

"It is my business, Sage, 'cause I'm in love wit' you..."

She rolled her eyes. "Here we go..."

"Fuck you mean, here we go?"

"I already told you what it is, so catching any kind of feelings for me is on you! Why are you making it more than what it is?" Shaking her hand, Sage decided to just close the door and leave that crazy nigga out there to look like a damn fool.

He wasn't having it, because he stuck his Polo booted foot in the way, so she couldn't close the door. "Move your foot before I break it," Sage warned meaning it with all her heart.

"Break it then. You already broke my heart, so that's nothing."

"Are you serious?" Sage shook her head and looked back at Danielle who was standing right behind her.

"Should I call the cops?" Her voice was a whisper but full of alarm.

Shaking her head, Sage assured her that it wasn't that serious. "Nah, girl, he's about to leave."

"I'm gonna leave, but I'll be back. If you don't want to deal with me, you better move," he threatened through clenched teeth before walking off.

Not able to believe how Bryan had gone from cool with their situation to a stalker in no time, Sage chalked it off as a young dude who was just whipped. He'd get over it, she thought as she closed the door. At least he went to Morehouse, and she didn't have to take any classes with him. As far as moving, she took his threat lightly. What was he really going to do?

Chapter 3

Vintage was so tired of Sage trying to find love for her when she couldn't maintain a stable relationship herself. That girl was a real ho, and she knew it. With a sly smile, Vintage had exchanged numbers with the handsome stranger, but she didn't let her sister know. Maybe it was best that she kept it to herself. Vintage felt that when her excitement got the best of her, and she let others in on what was going on things always went left.

"Hi, Stone" He'd wasted no time calling her. As a matter of fact, it was the next day.

"I hope I'm not ruining your first impression of me." With a nervous chuckle, he added, "I'm not really good with words."

"You're not, and it's okay as long as your words aren't lies." As soon as it escaped her lips, Vintage wondered if what she had said was inappropriate. She didn't want to make him think she was holding on to bad feelings from a previous relationship, although she was.

"I don't have a reason to lie to you. To be completely honest with you, when I saw you, I thought you were gorgeous and here we are." He sounded sincere, but Vintage wasn't convinced.

"Okay, but I'm just getting out of a relationship, so at this point all I really want is... a friend, I guess. I don't want to rush into anything." Vintage didn't have many friends. She was close to Sage, and her only best friend lived more than six hundred miles away in Virginia. Casey had gotten married a year ago and had a baby girl on the way. Not an envious person, Vintage longed for what she had.

"Are you okay?" Stone sounded concerned as he asked. "You act like I just asked you to marry me, and I just met you."

"I'm so sorry if I came off that way." She had to curse herself for taking it that far with him. He was being the perfect gentleman, and she was being a rambling fool. "You are right. I'm thinking way too far ahead. Sorry."

Stone chuckled good-naturedly. "It's fine. I understand where you're coming from, and I'm down for taking things slow. As a matter-of-fact, all I want right now is to get to know you. Is that okay?"

"Yes, that's perfect." Forcing a smile on her face, although he couldn't see her, Vintage decided to not overthink things. They were merely two people having a phone conversation, nothing more and nothing less.

After talking for over two hours, she learned a lot about Stone. He was twenty-three and single with no kids. That was a relief. One thing she wasn't willing to deal with was "baby mama" drama. All men with children didn't have those problems, but from what she knew, most did. He'd also just received his BS from Georgia State in Accounting and worked for an accounting firm in downtown Atlanta. He was a professional man, not a gamer, and she was ready to deal with a man who was on the same maturity level that she was.

"So, Vintage, I'm really enjoying our conversation. You're a breath of fresh air. Not only are you intelligent, but I love your sense of humor. You have this... innocence about you that I like. I hope it's not an act."

That made her giggle. "One thing I'm bad at is acting, so what you see is what you get."

"Good. How about I take you out to dinner on Friday night, so we can continue this face to face."

Without hesitation, she took him up on his offer. What would it hurt? She was single now and free to date if she chose. The relationship with Joshua had taught her one thing. Often, a woman would leave a relationship mentally before she actually left physically. What they had was over a long time ago.

* * *

Vintage's first date with Stone had started out great. After a delicious dinner at The Sundial, they went to a sip and paint event. With a glass full of Chardonnay, she attempted to paint a sophisticated melanin queen who was wearing a big hat. With his vodka and cranberry juice, Stone painted a beautiful ocean sunset with seagulls flying along the horizon. His was actually good, but Vintage thought her painting sucked.

"Why are you looking at your painting like that?" he asked with one eyebrow raised.

"It's horrible." With a laugh she shook her head, seeming tipsy.

"No, it's not. You're just feeling that wine." Stone flashed a sexy smile her way.

The man was so fine, her heart started to flutter. With smooth, milk chocolate skin and hazel eyes, he was definitely some eye candy. Not as tall as she was used to, he was only 5'11. That was tall enough for her though. Dimples and thick lips made her weak along with his athletic build. It was clear that he had a nice chest and six-pack under his black Ralph Lauren button down.

The sound of Vintage's phone chiming let her know that she had a notification of some kind, but she ignored it. It was her first date with Stone, and she didn't want to be all rude on her phone. Besides, it wasn't like he was checking his. Suddenly, he glanced over at her. "I think I had one drink too many. I'll be back. Gotta make a restroom run."

After he strolled off, she picked her phone up to see why it was chiming over and over. When she saw that it was an Instagram notification, she clicked on it and what she saw made her jaw drop.

"Nooo..." she screeched as the short video played, mocking a moment in time.

She'd once sent Joshua a video of her flashing her breasts. Although they had never had actual sex, Vintage had made attempts to be sexy for him. Obviously, he saw it as her just being a tease. The caption for the video was, *Look at this virgin dick teaser.*

Tears burned her eyes as she tried to delete the post but couldn't. He would have to the one to delete it, or she could report the post as abuse. Quickly reporting the post, she felt the hotness on her cheeks. Why was he doing that to her? Was he trying to sabotage her? Sending him a quick direct message, she let him know that he was out of line for posting something so personal. If he was in his feelings that was fine, but why was he coming at her like he wasn't the cheater?

Before Vintage could wipe her tears away, Stone was standing beside her. Looking at her with concern in his eyes, he lifted her chin. "Are you crying?"

Shaking her head, Vintage denied it. "No, I got something in my eye."

"Why do I not believe that? What happened that fast?" His concern really touched her, but she didn't want to come off as so... vulnerable.

With a sigh, she went ahead and told him the truth. "Well, my ex posted a private video that I sent him on Instagram. Uh, I..." Lowering her voice, she continued. "I'm a... virgin. He accused me of being a tease and..."

"What?"

"I'm a virgin and..."

"I heard that part," Stone spoke up. "I'm shocked that he would do something like that. Hurt people tend to hurt people, baby girl. He is mad because he wasn't able to be the one to... deflower you."

"Deflower?" His choice of words made her laugh.

"I'm trying to be tactful," he assured her with a smile. "You don't deserve being exposed like that, but you can't let him get to you. Embrace it. I'm sure you have nice breasts." With a shrug, he went back to painting.

"So, if you sent a chick a pic of your penis, would you be okay with her sharing it with everybody on social media?" Vintage quizzed him.

"I'm packing something, so yeah. Why be mad? If anything, it's some woman out there who's going to shoot her shot. This will have the reverse effect for him. Instead of dudes being mad, they are going to be intrigued by the beautiful virgin with the nice breasts."

"You're a trip." Vintage wiped the tears from her eyes.

"I'm just telling the trutd, but it is what it is. I'm sure you look amazing on that video, so don't trip about it. When he sees that it doesn't bother you, I'm sure he'll leave you alone and move on with his life."

She bit down on her bottom lip in contemplation. "I hope so, but I'm worried that this will mess up my business, you know?"

"Look, it's not that serious. People send videos and pics like that to their significant other every day. You haven't done anything that nobody else does. It's all good. He's bitter, so the best thing for you to do is show him that you're moving on from the bullshit."

With a nod, Vintage knew that he was right. Her tears were dry, and she realized that Joshua was probably helping her business instead of hurting it. "Controversy sells, right?"

Stone agreed. "Yes, it does. You're sexy and breasts are a beautiful, natural thing."

They both laughed.

"I still hope he deletes it. It's embarrassing." She shook her head before putting the finishing touches on her painting. It actually wasn't that bad. Trying to distract herself, she couldn't help but think about how Josh was trying his best to ruin her life. What would he be capable of doing next?

"He only did that because he knows what he let go. He lost you and that's the simple truth. Don't let him win. As a matter-of-fact, you should make a comment under the post letting all your new fans know that you embrace your body, beauty, and sexuality. Don't let him win," Stone suggested.

He was on to something. With a sly grin, Vintage pulled out her phone and assessed the Instagram page. Without giving it much thought, she started typing. Adding smiley emojis and hearts, she commented, *I love myself and if you did, you wouldn't be bitter enough to post this. I'm looking good, I must admit. Don't you agree?*

Smiling down at her, Stone asked, "Don't you feel better now?"

"Honestly, I do." Vintage returned his smile and allowed him to plant a sweet kiss on the tip of her nose.

"Good," he remarked before finishing off his drink. "You want another one?"

"Hell yeah, but are you okay to drive? Uh, we shouldn't both be drunk."

Stone shook his head. "I can handle my alcohol, beautiful. Relax."

"Done," she confirmed with a nod.

Watching him walk away, she was taken by his confidence and swag. He'd changed her bad mood and hadn't judged her. What really impressed her was the fact that he didn't question her virgin status. It didn't seem to faze him one way or the other. He was into her and her lack of sexual experience didn't matter. That was refreshing, and Vintage couldn't help but notice Stone's potential.

He returned with their drinks and passed her the glass of wine. "A toast to new beginnings and accepting the fact that life is too short to sweat the small stuff."

"I'll drink to that," Vintage clinked her glass against his before taking a long sip.

* * *

Vintage badly wanted to tell Sage about her date with Stone. She didn't though, and when Sage called her, she pretended to not be interested in the "sexy" man who was Stone.

"I saw Josh's post. The nerve of his ass!" Her anger was apparent. "How do you want to handle him?"

"The post has been deleted, and I'm over it. Did you see the comments?" Vintage laughed.

"Umm..." Sage sounded stunned. "You're taking that shit better than I thought."

"Yeah, well, my breasts did look good, so..."

Laughing, Sage had to admit that she was noticing a subtle change in her otherwise shy sister. "What? They did look good and all, but are you really okay after he pulled that stunt?"

"Yeah, I'm over it. He's bitter, but I'm not. He lost me, and this is his way of dealing with it." Brushing it off, Vintage wasn't really that convinced, but Stone's words resonated with her.

"Hmm... why the change of heart about that type of stuff? Have you met somebody?" Sage asked.

"I bet your eyes are all narrow and your face is balled up." Vintage laughed. "When I meet somebody worth my time, you'll be the first to know, sister."

"Yeah, I know, but what about the fine ass dude who was at the gala? He was on you, bih. I hope you at least gave him your number. If you didn't you're a fuckin' fool, and I'm disowning your ass."

Vintage broke out into uncontrollable laughter. "I can't even keep it from you, Sage. I did give him my number, and we went out on Friday."

"So, you went out with him and didn't even tell me? What the hell kind of sister are you? You got secrets now? Wow! Who are you?"

Vintage downplayed her sister's reaction. "I didn't want to tell you because I feel like I'm cursed or something when it comes to love. I didn't want to put my mouth on it and jinx it before it could even happen. We had dinner at the Sundial then did a sip and paint. That was when I saw Josh's post. I was upset, and Stone noticed."

"That's his name?"

"Yup, Stone Phillips."

"Strong name," Sage pointed out. "Continue."

"Well, he told me to embrace it, and maybe he's right. I've been on that uptight shit all my life. It's time for a change."

"Yes! Thank you! It took a new man to convince you of that when I've been telling you the same thing for years. I ain't trippin' though. Do your thing, sis! I like this new attitude and all, but damn, you should've been made this change. You can be quite boring," Sage quipped.

"Kiss my ass, Sage. You be on some judgmental mess, for real. Anyway, I'm good over here. You're the one who be putting yourself in complicated situations. What's up with Bryan?"

"You would rub that in, wouldn't you?" Vintage could see Sage rolling her eyes in annoyance. "Things have been quiet. He was just talking."

"But you can't be sure of that," Vintage pointed out.

"I'm sure of it. Bryan isn't some thug or anything. He's the captain of the football team, and he got a full scholarship. He has too much to lose, so I'm not worried." Sage tried to downplay the situation, but Vintage knew better.

"Wake up lil' sis. He's a football player and he may have suffered from concussions. You never know what state his brain is in. Just be careful. If something happened to you, I don't know what I'd do. You're all I have." For years Vintage had been worried about how loose her sister was with men.

"You're stressing for nothing, Vin. I got this." Sage laughed it off. "You know me. I am not the one to just let my guard down. Pops taught us to stay strapped. I'll shoot first and ask questions last. Pipe down. You think I'm soft or something?"

"No, I just think you're human. You're not invincible, Sage. You know what happened to ma and daddy."

"You don't have to remind me. 'Til this day, I wonder how they let that happen. How did they get so comfortable? I mean, daddy had to know that he had enemies and..."

"They were obviously asleep, Sage. You can't be on guard when you're sleeping. You're really blaming them for getting killed?" Vintage couldn't believe her sister felt that way because she'd never expressed that before.

"I'm not blaming them. I just wish daddy had done something. If only he'd known and stopped it. I miss them so much, Vin. I think that's why love is the furthest thing from my mind. It's so hard for me to attach." She sniffed in an attempt to hold back the tears.

"I understand, and it's probably the opposite for me. It's like I want love so bad to fill that void. It's like the thought of babies makes me happy, because we need to expand our family. We don't really have anybody but us, Sage. We've been through a lot, but it's time to move on."

"Easier said than done." Sage let out a sigh. "I gotta go, sis, but I'll call you back later."

"What do you have going on?"

"Finishing up the catalog. I'm shocked you didn't bring it up."

"Oh, for once work is the furthest thing from my mind."

Sage expressed her surprise. "Oh my, hell's going to freeze over. You're not thinking of work?"

"Shut up. I'm going to call you later on. Love you, Sage."

"Love you more, Vin."

Chapter 4

Sage stood and wiped her mouth as Jose visibly shivered from the aftershocks of the pleasure she'd just put down on him. They'd only been messing around for a few months, but Sage wasn't really one to hold anything back in the bedroom. Oral sex wasn't really sacred to her and had been the first sexual act she'd indulged in before losing her virginity.

Making her way to the master bath, she grabbed a washcloth from the linen closet and lathered it up with soap and water. She strolled back to the bed, letting her hips sway. Jose was shaking his head at her as she approached him.

"Mmm, I'm so glad your fine ass came over. You're everything, Sage, for real."

Jose was Puerto-Rican and a big drug dealer. Sage was addicted to having sex with thugs. She'd especially never get serious about a street dude though. The risks were too great, and she didn't want to meet the same fate her mother had.

Wiping the semen away that she'd made sure hit his thigh instead of her taste buds, Sage smiled down at him sexily. "I'm glad I came over too, baby. Hmm... I'm still tingling from all those orgasms. Roll a blunt. I'm trying to get high before we tear it up in here for real."

"I need a damn Red Bull and a Viagra to keep up wit' yo' ass." Jose laughed as he sat up and grabbed the bag of weed and Swisher from the nightstand.

Sage let out a giggle. "If it's too much for you, let me know, baby. I'm sure it's a man out there who can handle it."

"Oh, hell nah, I ain't complaining. I'm tryna keep all that for myself, ma. For real. I'on like to share. I'm stingy. You feel me?" His eyes searched hers as he broke the weed up in the blunt.

"Uh, so what makes you think you're the only one? I mean, you haven't made an attempt to commit to me."

Not that she wanted him to, but she had to make it clear that neither of them had made any claim on the other.

"I'm just lettin' you know what's up." As he licked the blunt, Sage couldn't help but press her thighs together. That man knew exactly what to do with that long tongue of his. Flashbacks of how he'd sucked the pure life out of her earlier made her feel the wetness gather between her thighs again.

Jose wasn't really the affectionate, touchy-feely type, which was more than cool with Sage. That was how she preferred things anyway. Without him even having to tell her, she knew what kind of man he was. Not caring about it, she was aware that he had other women that he was dealing with. Why did he think she'd only deal with him?

"What you thinkin' 'bout?" Jose passed Sage the blunt.

"Why're you trying to pick my brain?" She didn't really want to get deep with him at the moment. All she wanted was to get her back banged out and go home.

"Well, we been fuckin' for a while, and that's all we do. Even somebody like me likes to talk to the woman I'm in bed with. Why not, since you're here."

"Since I'm here?" Sage snickered and blew the smoke out of her nose. "Wow. Don't worry about my brain. That's the part of my body that should be the least of your concern."

"You're so much like a man, for real." Jose took the blunt from Sage's outstretched fingers and took a pull. "Can't nobody tame you, huh?"

"Tame me? If that's your plan give up now." Getting up from the bed, she decided to put her clothes on and just leave. She could do without feeling something hard and real for the night. Her mind was on the many gadgets in her toy box. The thought of the new Jack Rabbit that she'd bought made her grin from ear to ear in anticipation.

"What you doin'?" Jose asked as she got dressed.

"I'm getting dressed," she told him nonchalantly.

"Why? You don't need clothes for what we're about to do." The scowl on his face made Sage laugh out loud.

"In case you don't get the hint, we're not about to do a damn thing. I'm going home." Once she was fully dressed, she headed toward the door without looking back.

Grabbing her by the wrist, Jose spun her around to face him. "What's your problem?"

"I don't have a problem, but if you don't get your hands off me, you will!" Sage snapped with her eyes wide.

Jose let her go, but she could tell that his ego was bruised for some reason. It wasn't like she was his woman and they should have pillow talk. All she wanted to do was sex him, smoke and go home. Why did men have to make things so difficult? If she was the one so ready to commit and be serious, he'd be running for the hills. It was such a double standard.

"I'm sorry. Look, just chill out. I don't want you to leave. As a matter of fact, I want to do more than what we've been doing. I be wanting to take you out, but you're the one who wants to just lay up. Why are you like that? I mean, I love sex too, but damn, you're the type of woman that a man wants more with. It's like you try your best to make that shit hard. Explain it to me." His eyes pleaded with her, but she was defiant as always.

"I don't have to explain anything to you, Jose. I don't owe you anything. As a matter of fact, if you must know, I only want to lay up with you. I don't want anything else. What can you possibly offer me other than some temporary fairytale? With the lifestyle you live it's only two ways out, and that's a jail cell or a grave. I'm not setting myself up to be with a man who'll be taken away from me. Nope... not doing it, so I enjoy your body and I keep my mind and heart separate. Men do it all the time." Sage shrugged. "Why is it an issue when a woman does it?"

"Just go ahead and leave, Sage. I'm clearly wasting my time." Jose turned and walked off.

"Good, bye!" As she left, she felt a twinge of guilt in her heart. Jose wasn't a bad guy. She just didn't want to face the fact that she may have felt something for him, even if it wasn't that strong. Whatever spark she may experience when it came to a man was extinguished by her doubts before it could grow into a full inferno. In Sage's opinion, that was best for her.

* * *

Bobbing her head to Cardi B's "I Like It Like That", Sage was so caught up in the music's vibe that she didn't even notice the dark colored car following close behind her. By the time her eyes caught the bright glare of the headlights, it was too late for her to comprehend what was really going on.

"What the hell? Why are they following me so close?" she asked out loud before turning the loud music down.

Hitting the gas, Sage figured it was just somebody who didn't know how to drive. Or maybe she was going too slow, and that was their hint for her to speed up. Turning the radio back up, she rapped along with Cardi just as the same car started to increase its speed and tail her again.

Not even five minutes from her subdivision, she was pissed off that somebody was trying her patience. Throwing up the bird out of the window at the driver behind her, she wanted to curse him or her out, but of course, they wouldn't hear her. "Just go around me, bitch!" she screamed in annoyance.

Squinting her eyes, she tried to make out what kind of car it was, but the headlights were so bright they were blinding. There was no way she could even make out the color of the car let alone the make and model.

When she felt her bumper being slightly hit by the car, she realized that shit had just got real. Mad as hell, she could feel her temper boiling to the surface. Before she could pull her car over to assess the damage, the car hit her in the back hard as hell. The impact caused her vehicle to go into a tailspin.

In an attempt to gain control of the car, Sage gripped the steering wheel. Taking her foot off the gas, she knew better than to accelerate and pumped the brakes in a panic. That was when she realized that her brakes weren't working.

"Fuck!" she screeched just as she slammed into the back of a car in front of her. That car started to spin and hit her again from the side. By that time, even with her seatbelt on, Sage was being thrown around like a rag doll. Her face had already slammed into the steering wheel and as darkness engulfed her, her car continued to careen down the road until it crashed head first into a tree.

* * *

It was after four am when Vintage's phone rang. In a deep slumber, she didn't even hear it at first. As her eyes fluttered open, she grabbed the phone from her nightstand and tried to make out the name on the screen. It was Danielle, so she answered knowing that something had to have happened to Sage. Her heart immediately dropped to her feet.

"Hello?"

"Vintage, it's Danielle. You have to come to Grady now. Sage was in a car accident."

"Is she alive?" Vintage jumped up to throw something on. Panic took over as she tried to keep the tears at bay.

"Yes, but you have to get here. She's been hurt really badly," Danielle explained.

"Okay, I'm on my way." Slipping her feet into some comfortable slide-ins, Vintage was rushing toward the door with her purse in hand.

In a daze, she got behind the wheel of her car and headed to the hospital. On the way, she said a prayer for her sister knowing that if something happened to her, she'd never be the same again.

* * *

Rushing into the hospital's entrance, Vintage headed straight to the front desk. "My sister was in an accident. Her name is Sage Saldana. Please, I have to see her."

The front desk receptionist pressed some keys on the computer's keyboard before looking up at Vintage. "She's in surgery right now, but someone will be out to speak with you soon."

"Vintage," Danielle muttered behind her before reaching out to give her a hug.

"They wouldn't tell me much, because I'm not family. Hopefully, somebody will be out to give us an update soon."

Holding on to Danielle, Sage finally let it all out. "If she doesn't make it, I don't know what I'll do."

Soothingly rubbing her back, Danielle assured her that Sage would be okay. "One thing about your sister is, she's a fighter. She's going to be fine, Vintage. We both have to think positive."

Taking in a breath, Vintage got herself together and pulled away from Danielle. "You're absolutely right. Sage has way too much to get into. She'll never give up that easily."

"Exactly." Danielle and Vintage both sat down and tried to wait it out for someone to give them some news.

Almost two hours had passed by before a doctor finally approached them. "Miss Saldana's family?"

"Yes," Vintage confirmed as she stood to her feet.

"I'm Doctor Chandler," he introduced himself.

Vintage couldn't care less what his name was. "Is my sister okay?"

"She's resting, and she's stable. There're no serious internal injuries, but we're keeping an eye on her in case anything changes. We had to do surgery because her femur was shattered into pieces. It's touch and go at this point, but there's a chance that she will not gain full usage of her leg. Then again, things could go a different way. She's badly bruised, and her jaw had to be wired shut. There's slight brain swelling, so we have to keep an eye out for brain damage. She's being transferred to a room in ICU. A nurse will be out shortly, so you can see her. She's heavily sedated and not responding right now, so be prepared."

"Do you think she's going to make it?" Vintages voice cracked at the thought of burying her only sister.

Knowing that her grandparents were on the way to the hospital was enough for her. All they had was their father's parents because their mother's parents had passed away when they were younger.

"Yes, at this point her chance of survival is very high, but you must be prepared for anything." The doctor's eyes were sincere, but it wasn't exactly what Vintage wanted to hear.

"Thank you, doctor," she simply stated before pacing the floor nervously.

Danielle had heard everything the doctor said and wiped tears from her eyes as she excused herself. "I have to make a phone call, Vintage. I'll be right back. I'm not leaving your side. Sage is like my sister too."

"I know, Danielle. Thank you."

 Less than thirty minutes later a nurse came to usher Vintage to Sage's room. She had heeded the doctor's warning but still wasn't prepared for what she saw. Her sister's face was so badly swollen and bruised that she didn't even recognize her. Swallowing the lump in her throat, she tried her best not to cry.

"Sage," she whispered holding on to her limp hand. "I'm here, and I'm not leaving until you wake up."

The steady beeping of the heart monitor was the only comfort that Vintage had of her sister being alive. From looking at her, there were no real signs of life. There were all types of tubes coming from her orifices, and she was as still as a board. The subtle up and down motion of her chest was the only proof that Sage was breathing.

Vintage took in a deep breath. "Grandma and grandpa will be here soon. Don't worry, Sage. You're going to make it through this. You have to fight. I love you so much and..."

There was a tap at the door and when Vintage looked back, she was face to face with two detectives. It brought back déjà vu of when her parents were murdered. Why were they there for a car accident?

"Vintage Saldano?" One of them asked. He was a tall, light-skinned man with a receding hairline and average features.

"Yes?"

"I'm Detective Rolling and this is Detective Harmon. We are here to investigate your sister's... incident." He walked into the room followed by the younger, chestnut brown skinned detective.

"Okay, but why are you here? My sister was in a car accident." Vintage's confusion was apparent.

"We are aware of that, but witnesses have a different story. A witness called 911 and reported that someone ran into your sister on purpose. It was a black Charger that was involved. Once your sister's car spun out of control, the driver simply drove off. Is there anyone who would want to hurt her that you know of?"

Bryan was the first person to come to Vintage's mind, but with Sage's history, it could've been anybody. Not wanting to tarnish her sister's reputation, she didn't know how to respond. "Well, uh, I don't know who would want to hurt her, but..."

"But what? Does she have a boyfriend?" Detective Harmon seemed anxious for answers.

"Well, no, but... she has a couple men that she..." Vintage couldn't find the right words to describe it.

"Oh, so your sister plays the field," Detective Harmon attempted to confirm.

"Well, she is nineteen and single. I mean, she's young. What's wrong with that?" Vintage didn't want them judging Sage. They'd already had awful experiences when it came to the police, so why would that be any different? Now that her sister was the victim, it didn't really seem to matter.

"Nothing, we just need you to give us any information that you may have, so we can solve this alleged crime. It appears that somebody wanted to hurt your sister, and you can help us find them." Detective Rolling passed me a business card. "If you can recall anything specific call me. We would love to speak to your sister too. Her car is being investigated. One of the witnesses stated that it appeared as if her brakes didn't work. Her cellphone was found, and first responders called the first number that they found in her car log. We also have her phone for evidence. The only thing we are concerned about is finding out who did this to your sister. We'd hate for them to try again."

With a nod, Vintage had to agree. "I feel the same way, and I'll get my sister to contact you. Of course, she knows more about her personal life than I do."

The detectives left, and Vintage was relieved. Her pain ran deep, and although it wasn't like her, she wanted some vengeance of her own. She was tired of others taking those that she loved away from her. If she found out who had tried to kill her sister, she wasn't going to wait for the cops to handle it. The way she felt at that moment, she was ready to murder somebody herself.

Chapter 5

"Are you okay, Vintage?" Stone asked when he finally heard her voice on the line.

"No," she sniffed. "My sister was in a car accident last night that doesn't really look like an accident according to the police."

"What? Is she okay?" Stone's voice was filled with concern as he asked.

"Not really, but she will be. At least I pray that she will. Sage is vain, and I have no idea how things will play out." Vintage sighed heavily. "I don't know how to feel right now."

"Are you at the hospital now?"

"No, I just got home. I had to shower and change clothes. I need to eat too, but I can't. I haven't slept. This is too much. My sister means the world to me. Thank God she woke up because I was determined to stay at that hospital until she opened her eyes."

"I love how close you two are. I'm an only child, so I kind of missed that bond growing up. How about I come pick you up and take you to get something to eat? Then I'll take you back to the hospital. I'll patiently wait for you to see your sister and then take you home. You shouldn't be driving yourself around right now. I'm here for you, Vintage."

"I appreciate it, Stone, I really do... but..."

"No buts," he spoke up. "I won't take no for an answer. Now, I'm off today, and I'm at your beck and call. I don't mind. As a matter of fact, I want to be there for you."

"Aww, Stone, that's so sweet. Okay. I'll be ready when you get here." She obliged feeling relieved to know that somebody was there for her. It felt so good to know that he wanted to make himself available when she needed him the most. Vintage was impressed.

* * *

"If you don't want to talk about it, it's fine, but why do they think what happened to your sister wasn't an accident?" Stone asked as they feasted on chicken and waffles and Nana G's. The soul food was off the chain, and it wasn't too far from the hospital.

"Witnesses say that somebody ran her off the road in a black Charger. When Sage woke up, she wasn't really responsive, and I didn't want to bombard her with questions. She's been through enough. My sister is nothing like me, Stone. She's more... free-spirited for lack of a better word. She's the social butterfly, and she loves men. I'm wondering if she broke the wrong heart, you know? Women aren't the only ones who become scorned." That was obvious with how Joshua was handling their break up. Thankfully, she hadn't had any more problems out of him. Maybe Stone was right about her pretending to not be bothered. So far, she was leaving her alone.

"People are unpredictable. You have to be careful. A few years back, I was dealing with this chick, but it really wasn't serious. I had told her that I wasn't ready to be in a relationship. At the time, I had just started taking the

85

hardest classes toward my degree. I had to focus. She

didn't understand my ambition and started acting like

she was on some stalker shit. After a while, she moved

on, but it was crazy at first. She busted the windows out

of my car and everything."

That made Vintage think about Jazmine Sullivan's

song, "I Busted the Windows Out Your Car." That was

her joint and as the lyrics played in her mind, she

thought about what kind of revenge she'd get on the

person that hurt her sister. Then she thought about what

she'd do if she found out who had executed her parents.

"You finished eating?" Stone asked when he noticed

that she wasn't touching her food. "If you want, you can

take the rest with you. I'm sure you're anxious to get back

to your sister."

"I am." Vintage stared at him, wondering if he had an

agenda. Could a man really be that kind and genuine?

"Thank you for being so thoughtful."

"You don't have to thank me for doing what I want to

do, baby girl. I'm telling you now, as time goes on, you'll

see that all I want to do is make sure you're good, friend or whatever."

"And I appreciate that. There aren't many genuine people out here anymore. It's like when you meet somebody new, you're always taking a chance. I'm not like my sister in that way. I'm not the one who feels comfortable taking chances. Now, I don't know... I'm thinking that my way may be stifling me. I mean, I'm not ever going to be as open as Sage, but I can balance it all out. I want to enjoy life for once. I want to stop and smell the flowers, but I can't do that if my sister isn't okay. She's all I have, Stone."

"And you still have her. She's still here, and I'm sure that with you in her corner supporting her, she'll make a full recovery. Although I haven't known you that long, you have me too, Vintage. I'm not going anywhere anytime soon. So, you might as well get used to me being around." Stone grinned, exposing his straight, white teeth.

Vintage didn't flinch when he said that. Against her will, she welcomed his willingness to give her a shoulder to lean on. She really needed it, so she didn't decline his offer. Maybe it was time for her to let a man take charge and be there for her. She'd always avoided letting someone care for her because she didn't want to depend on something that wasn't stable. Stability was something she longed for since she'd never really had it.

After Stone paid for their dinner, they headed to his car. On the way to the hospital, neither of them really said much. Vintage was so lost in her thoughts and all Stone could think about was the beautiful woman that he now found himself smitten with.

* * *

"I look horrible," Sage whined when she was finally able to look at herself in a mirror.

After a few days, she'd been moved from the ICU to a regular room. A couple of her front teeth were knocked out, and she would eventually have to have reconstructive surgery to repair the damage to her face.

"Don't let your vanity trump the fact that you are still alive," Vintage reminded Sage.

"Okay, I'm alive, but look at me, Vin. I look like shit." Sage sobbed, and her body shook as she came to grips with her new reality. "My leg is busted all up, and I may have a fuckin' limp for the rest of my life."

"But at least you have the rest of your life. Would you rather have died than be going through this because if so, that's some selfish shit."

"Why?" Sage's bloodshot eyes were on Vintage. "Because you need me here for you? Look at you. You're still perfect, but look at me."

Vintage shook her head. "Are you serious right now? That's how you feel, Sage? You're really that weak? I never thought I'd see the day that you'd put your beauty over your life. You will get that back, Sage. They're going to do the surgery tomorrow and when you heal, you will look like your normal self. Why is that so important though?"

"Because my looks are my life. You know that." The tears rolled down her puffy cheeks.

Gently wiping them away for Sage, Vintage leaned over and wrapped her arms around her. "I love you. I don't want you to give up now. You've come too far."

"I love you too, and I... I'm sorry. It's just... I don't know who did this to me. I'm all fucked up." Sage's lips trembled as she tried to hold new tears back.

"Those detectives want to talk to you soon." Vintage had already filled her in on the fact that what had happened to her was no accident.

Sage already knew that, but she had no idea who the culprit was. After the police investigated her vehicle it was discovered that her brake line had been cut. That meant that the person who ran her off the road knew that she wouldn't be able to stop. That was definitely attempted murder.

"I still can't think of anybody who drives a black Charger," Sage pointed out. "Bryan drives a dark blue Mustang."

"You don't just deal with him. What do the other dudes you're sleeping with drive?" Vintage didn't mean to pry. She just wanted to be able to exact revenge for her sister.

Sage looked pissed off. "Don't judge me."

"I'm not. I just want to figure out who did this, so it won't happen again."

"You're always judging me, and you know it, Vin." Sage's voice was weak but full of conviction.

"That's not true, Sage. You're who you are, and I'm who I am. Just because we're different doesn't mean I feel some type of way about it. To be honest, I envy you."

"For real?" Sage's eyes seemed to come to life. "Because I envy you too."

"Why?" Vintage was surprised to hear her sister say that. She'd always thought Sage was more beautiful. Her caramel complexion was so flawless and smooth with a splash of freckles across her nose. Her wild, curly hair was unruly and edgy, and she didn't mind wearing her real hair. Her nose was round at the tip and cute to

Vintage. She hated her own pointy nose. Her sister's figure was long and slim, like a supermodel's. She still managed to have a nice, round booty and C-cup breasts though. The slim twenty-four-inch waistline of hers was snatched and Vintage knew that was why she got so much male attention.

"Because you've always been perfect, inside and out. I'm ugly now, Vin. Nobody's going to want me," Sage whispered.

"That's not true, and I don't want to hear you say that again. You're beautiful and you always will be. Beauty is within, Sage. It's not just the outside..."

"That's easy for you to say, Vin." Sage closed her eyes. "Can you go home, please. I need some rest."

"You really want me to leave?" Vintage sounded hurt but knew that her sister was just going through the motions.

"I'm going to still have a broken leg and face tomorrow, so it doesn't matter." With that said, she pretended to be asleep.

Instead of leaving like Sage had asked her to, Vintage sat there. Like she's promised before, she wasn't going to leave her side until she woke up. This time, it was more than her unconscious self that Vintage was waiting to see submerge. She needed her sister to experience a mental awakening that would make all the superficial stuff obsolete.

* * *

"You okay? You haven't said more than two words since we left the hospital," Stone spoke up a few minutes after he drove off.

"I'm sorry. It's a lot on my mind. That's all."

Stone put his hand on her knee and squeezed. "Do you want to talk about it?"

"No, actually, I don't," she admitted.

"Okay, I can respect that, but if you want to... talk, I'm here."

"I thought you weren't good with words."

"I'm not, but I can listen."

Vintage could appreciate that because sometimes that was all she needed. An ear was all she wanted with no judgment or advice. All she wanted was to vent and purge her feelings. Over the years, she'd become so good at hiding them, she'd convinced herself that she was okay.

"I appreciate it, but all I want is to get some rest. I'm tired." Looking out of the window, Vintage just wanted to climb between her down comforter and Egyptian cotton sheets.

"Okay, I get it." Stone chuckled. "You need your space."

"Don't take it personally." She glanced over at him. "Thank you. I appreciate everything you've done for me."

"Whenever you need me, I'm here. No thanks needed."

For some reason, Vintage believed him.

* * *

A few weeks passed by and Sage's physical condition was improving. Her mental condition just seemed to be getting worse though. She would be released from the hospital in a few days, but Vintage thought she needed some type of therapy to deal with her mixed feelings.

Some dude named Jose had been to the hospital to visit her, and honestly, Vintage kind of liked him. He seemed to care for Sage, and Vintage wondered if she cared for him too. The question was, would she allow herself to feel something.

"So, you will be staying with me after you're discharged," Vintage told Sage as she opened the blinds in her room to let some sunlight in.

Sage had gone through reconstructive surgery and her teeth had been fixed, but her face was still red and puffy. "I know, Vin, but... I don't want you to treat me like I'm some kid or something." She shielded her eyes from the brightness.

Vintage ignored her sister's attitude. "Your physical therapy starts next week, and I don't want to hear any excuses. You don't want me to treat you like some kid, so get used to it."

"I can't move my leg, so what's the point?" Sage sounded defeated.

"The point is to use your leg again. See, here you go, but you won't be getting a pity party from me," Vintage told her sternly.

Letting out a deep, frustrated sigh, Sage rolled her eyes at Vintage. "It's not that I want a pity party. I just want to feel normal again, and the thought of getting out of her scares me. I don't know who did this, Vin. They questioned Bryan, but he doesn't have a black Charger. He denied being involved, and there's no evidence of him doing anything. Who the fuck could have cut my brake line and ran me off the road? It wasn't Jose, because he was still at home when it happened. That was proven because he was on his home computer looking at Porn Hub." His mind must've been on self-pleasuring too.

Vintage shook her head trying to stifle her laughter. "Porn Hub?"

Sage laughed for the first time in a while. "Yes, his alibi checked out because he was clearly watching porn at the time of my accident."

"It wasn't really an accident though," Vintage couldn't help but point out. "So, I feel your reluctance about getting out of here. You can't let whoever did this get the upper hand. We're going to find out who did it. In the meantime, I'm hiring security to keep an eye on you."

Sage looked at Vintage like she'd lost her mind. "I don't need security."

"Girl, you can save it. I'm not trying to hear it. Until whoever tried to kill you is caught, you will be watched like a hawk, understand?" Vintage's nostrils flared as she made herself clear.

"Yes, damn." Sage knew that her sister would be protective, but she'd taken things to a whole new level.

Looking up, Sage spotted Jose at the door. When a smile covered her face, Vintage glanced in the direction of her gaze. "Jose, hi," Vintage greeted him. "I was just about to leave. I have some business to attend to. You got her until I get back, right?"

"I sure do," he assured her with his eyes still on Sage. Not ever really feeling a woman in that way, although she'd rejected him, he still wanted to be with her.

Hopefully, he'd be able to prove his love in time. Sage wasn't the type to settle down so quickly, but he was determined to wear her down eventually. The right man was all she needed, and he was sure that she was his soul mate. Seeing her in such a vulnerable position pulled at his heartstrings, and he wasn't a soft dude. That was how he knew that what he felt for her was deeper than the physical.

Vintage kissed Sage on the forehead. "I'll be back in a few hours, okay?"

Sage nodded. "Okay. Love you, Vin."

"I love you more," Vintage confirmed before leaving her and Jose alone.

"I love you too, Sage," Jose finally admitted for the first time. "I know that scares you, but you can't push me away. I won't let you. I'm going to stick around and show you just how much I want and need you."

"This is not the time, Jose..."

He cut her off. "It *is* the time, Sage. You keep fighting what you feel, but why? Does the thought of being in love really scare of you that much? Since the day I found out you were hurt, I've been here. I don't care what the outcome is, I'm still here. That's because I actually give a fuck about you, no matter how much you push me away. You're worth loving, and I don't understand why you can't see that. Yeah, I fuck wit' other women, but that's only because you don't want to go there with me. I really want you, but you've made it clear over and over again that you don't do relationships."

The tears slid from Sage's eyes against her will. "You think you love me, but you don't, Jose. You love what I do to you. You love having sex with me. If you really had to deal with me, you'd feel differently. I know that because for some reason, my heart isn't really on the table. I can't explain it. Either way, keeping my feelings at bay is easier for me. Shit, it's easier for us both. I'm not who you think I am."

Jose laughed and grabbed Sage's hand. "What part of you can't push me away do you not understand? I swear you try your best to turn me off. I know exactly what kind of person you are. You think not loving me is best for you, because of what happened to your parents. I get it. You don't have to explain it to me. I'm the same way you are. I've always avoided love. You might not see it now, but in time, you'll see that we are meant to be together. Now, get some rest baby girl, and I'll be right here when you wake up."

The pain meds in the drip were working a number on her because although she was listening to Jose, she could barely keep her eyes open. Without bothering to respond to him, she felt herself being pulled into a deep, peaceful slumber.

Chapter 6

Sage had been out of the hospital for a couple weeks, and she was working Vintage's last nerve. "Why are you still in bed?" Vintage asked as she turned her bedroom light on. "You have physical therapy in thirty minutes."

"I'm not going." Sage pulled the cover over her head defiantly.

"Oh, yes the hell you are. Get your ass up." Vintage walked over and pulled the cover off her.

"Who do you think you are? You can't make me do a damn thing!" Sage's eyes were full of something that Vintage couldn't read.

"I don't even know who you are anymore. You're giving up, Sage. That's not like you. I thought you were the strong one. I guess I was wrong." Vintage shrugged and walked toward the door. "It's your leg, not mine. If you never want to walk again, that's on you."

"You're right. It's my leg, not yours! It's my life, not yours!" Sage lashed out with anger dripping from her words.

"Why are you mad at me though?" Vintage turned on her heels. "All I'm doing is trying to help your ass!"

"If you want to help me, then leave me alone!"

"That's really how you feel?" Vintage's eyes were like slits as she asked.

"Yes, I really mean it. I mean it with all my heart," Sage confirmed.

"Oh, you're really starting to piss me off, Sage! You're doing exactly what the person who did this to you wants! You're not the woman you once were, and in a way, I can understand. The thing is, you're not even trying. It's disappointing."

Sage looked Vintage right in the eye. "I don't care."

"I see that, and it's pathetic." Vintage left the bedroom and closed the door behind her.

Danielle had finished the catalog and thankfully, business was booming more than ever. That may have been due to the video that Joshua had posted. The result was totally different from what Vintage thought it would. Joshua had obviously moved on because in the past month he hadn't bothered her at all. She hadn't found his Burberry shirt either.

As far as Stone, they were seeing each other a lot and Vintage was starting to like him more and more. Not only was he attentive, but he was really a good listener. She'd tell him something and he'd recall it weeks later. That meant a lot to her. Of course, they hadn't had sex, but Stone made her feel ecstatic without her having an orgasm. In ways, she wanted to give herself to him, but she had to take her time. If she'd waited it out that long, she had to hold on and be strong-willed.

"Speaking of the devil," Vintage said out loud when her phone rang. There was a huge smile on her face.

"Hey Stone," she answered trying not to sound too anxious, but she was sure her voice gave her away.

"Hey, sweetness. I'm just calling to confirm our date tonight at nine. Are we still on?" He'd asked jokingly, so Vintage couldn't help but laugh.

"Of course, we're still on. I would have it no other way. So, where are we going?" she asked.

"It's a surprise, so I wish you'd stop asking. Just make sure you're dressed to kill. I'm sure that's not going to be a problem since you're always so immaculate." His deep voice was doing more to her than she wanted it to.

The heat that emanated between her thighs was something she'd rarely experienced. If she kept spending time with Stone, she felt that her weak side would come out. *You've held out this long, and you can keep on doing it until you get that ring*, she thought.

"Well, you know, it comes naturally," she joked, making light of the foul mood that she was really in.

As if he sensed something, Stone asked, "How's Sage doing?"

"She's being a real damn bitch," Vintage admitted. "She has physical therapy today, but she doesn't want to go. I've never seen her like this. It's like she's giving up. It's disheartening. She's usually the strong one."

"Well, maybe this happened for you to be the one that's strong. Maybe you'll be the one to help bring her out of this. Don't give up because she is. Show her that you can be the one to hold her up. You have to consider what's she's been through. Put yourself in her shoes."

When he said it, it made perfect sense to Vintage. "Why are you always able to show me such clarity?" It was crazy because she'd never met a man in her life with so much wisdom. "You're only twenty-three. Where did you come from?" she asked curiously.

Stone let out a light chuckle. "I'm just being me, gorgeous. Be you. You're way stronger than you think. That is clear. I see so much in you that I don't think you see. I'm just trying to figure out why you're blind to it. I see too many beautiful women like you who are the total package, and you bury yourselves in a hole hoping that nobody sees you at all. Too bad I'm the observant type. I don't care about those women who want to be seen so bad. I see way more in women like you. A buried treasure."

"Wow, but you said you're not good with words," Vintage pointed out.

"I'm not, but I don't mind telling it like it is."

"Thank you, Stone. I appreciate your honesty."

"And what did I tell you about thanking me."

"I know, but I just can't help it. Honesty is refreshing."

"Good. I'm glad. Now, I have to get back to work, baby. I'm sorry. I'll see you soon though. Stay pretty."

"And you stay handsome."

As Vintage ended the call, she couldn't help but actually smell Stone's Gucci Guilty cologne. "Mmmm," she said aloud as she shook her head.

The sound of Sage's voice interrupted her musing. "I'm ready to go since you insist."

She was standing at the top of the stairs fully dressed with that cast on her leg and crutches under her arms.

Vintage rushed to help her down the stairs. "That's what I'm talking about, Sage. Fear nothing."

"But God himself," Sage added as they made their way outside.

* * *

Sage was resting after a successful physical therapy session, and Vintage was taking a nice, bubble bath before her date with Stone. She knew that it was going to be a long process to get her sister back where she once was mentally and physically, but she was determined. She'd even looked into finding a therapist for her to talk to. Admittedly, she felt that she also needed to make an appointment for herself.

Sage would probably try to convince her that she was fine and didn't need to talk to anyone, but Vintage knew better. She'd lay it on her easily to not set her off. Maybe if Vintage offered to go to the sessions with her, she'd feel better about. In the black community mental health was often swept under the rug, but Vintage knew that it was just as important as physical health.

* * *

"Oh, wow... you look incredible." Stone grabbed Vintage's hand and kissed it, taking in the ravishing sight of her in her little, black dress.

"Thank you, Stone. You know you're looking like you stepped off the pages of GQ." He was decked out in a black Armani suit with a charcoal gray button-down underneath.

"Why, thank you. Shall we?" He tucked her arm into his.

"We shall."

Once they were in his car, Vintage couldn't help but try her luck. "So, where are we going?"

"Just sit back and ride, baby. You won't get me just because you're looking all lovely." There was a sly grin on his face that illuminated his handsome features.

"You're tough." Vintage laughed.

"That's true, but you bring out my soft side though. Just not this time." With a light chuckle, he pulled off.

Vintage shook her head and pretended to pout. Stone glanced over at her. "Aww, you look so cute, and I thought you were bad at acting."

"You can see right through me already, huh?" She giggled.

"Yup, clear as day." His hand was on her thigh, squeezing.

A shiver traveled over her being, but his touch didn't make her feel uncomfortable. Actually, it was welcomed, and she put her hand on top of his as they sped toward their destination.

* * *

"LocoLuna?" Vintage's stomach dropped. She hated nightclubs, and she'd told Stone that. Now it made sense to her why it was such a big secret. He knew that she'd never agree to go.

"It's salsa night," he sounded all happy about it, but Vintage wasn't a dancer. She'd sway to the beat of a song she liked, but that was about it.

"I don't dance, and I definitely can't do the salsa. Look, it's not too late for us to grab something to eat somewhere or..."

"We can eat here. They serve food. C'mon, Vintage. It'll be fun. Loosen up. You have that gorgeous body for a reason. You're black, so I know you got rhythm." Stone stared at her with convincing eyes.

"I told you that I don't do clubs, Stone. It's just not my... thing." She visibly shivered, but Stone was not to be deterred.

"How do you know if you don't like nightclubs if you don't go to them?" As he looked at her, he grabbed her hand. "Don't make me beg, because I will."

Vintage cracked a smile, challenging him.

"Please... Please... C'mon, please. I promise you'll enjoy yourself." As he pleaded, he held on to her hand, causing shock waves to travel other her nerve endings.

"Okay," she agreed with a reluctant shrug. "I guess it won't kill me. Don't laugh at my lack of dance skills."

"I'll teach you how to do the salsa. After we get full, we'll dance the night away. Get a few drinks in you, and you'll be tearing the floor up," he teased.

Vintage cracked up at the thought. "I seriously doubt it."

Before she could get the words out, Stone was out of the car and on her side opening the door. He helped her out of the car and waited for the valet attendant to come over and take his keys. Escorting her inside the club, like the perfect gentleman, he led her to the bar.

The crowd was a good size, but it was early, so it wasn't full to capacity yet. Vintage hated big crowds, although she often attended events. A regular club night was definitely not her routine, but like Stone had said, how could she knock something without trying it.

The colorful lights bounced off the walls and ceilings as high-energy Spanish music flowed from the loudspeakers.

"So, I take it that you've been here before," Vintage told Stone as she looked around and took in the scene.

"A few times," he told her as she sat down on the bar stool beside him.

"How's the food?"

"Really good and the drinks aren't watered down."

A bartender passed them both menus. "Can I get you two something to drink?" she asked, flipping her long, red hair over her shoulder.

"Yes, let me get a Long Island Iced Tea and..." He glanced over at Vintage.

"Let me get a sour apple martini."

"Okay, I'll make your drinks and give you some time to look over the menu."

"Thank you," Vintage and Stone said in unison.

"After a few of those strong ass martinis, you'll be on one of those poles." He glanced over at the two poles that were strategically placed on both sides of the dancefloor.

"It's too many cellphones up in here with cameras for me to do that. Last time I let my inhibitions go, I was exposed."

Stone shook his head. "You have to stop worrying about what other people think and enjoy your life."

Vintage sighed. "You sound just like Sage. I'm who I am, and if you don't like it..."

"I didn't say I don't like it. I actually love who you are as a person. You're sweet and genuine. I can see that you have a good heart. You're young though, and I just want you to live your life. Enjoy it. It's nothing wrong with doing things that make you uncomfortable. You might realize that you enjoy things you never thought you'd do." Stone's eyes were sincere as he continued. "You should make a list and check them off as you go."

"Like a bucket list?" Vintage scrunched up her nose as she asked.

"I guess you can say that." Soon the bartender was back with their drinks and Vintage hadn't even opened the menu yet.

"So, are you ready to order?"

"Give us a few more minutes," Stone spoke up.

"No problem," she nodded and walked off.

113

They both looked over the menu and Vintage ordered Spanish rice with Calamari. Stone ordered roast chicken with yellow rice and black beans. As they ate they exchanged a light banter, getting to know one another even more. Vintage was started to think that she could get used to Stone. Finally, she'd met a man who was close to her age, but in her league. Most men in their early twenties didn't exhibit the traits that he did.

Not only was Stone patient, but he was smart and hard-working. The fact that he was handsome as hell was a plus in Vintage's book. As she watched his thick lips while he talked and ate his food, she couldn't help but watch him lick his lips in longing. For a second, she didn't hear his words. She only saw his mouth moving, and it was a beautiful mouth.

"Mmm..." She didn't even realize that she'd let out that moan until Stone asked if her food was that good.

"Yes," she grinned. If only he knew that he looked that good.

Once they were finished eating, Stone flashed a questioning look her way. "You ready to dance."

"Not right now. I'm full." Actually, she was nervous and didn't want to look like a clumsy fool with two left feet. "How about another drink."

Stone signaled for the bartender to come over and ordered them another round. In no time, Vintage could feel herself relaxing and decided that she did want to dance. After her drink was gone, she was the one who grabbed Stone's hand and led him to the dancefloor.

"So, teach me how to do the salsa," she yelled over the music.

Stone shook his head. "You're looking way too good in that dress. Every man in here is looking at you."

Vintage looked around self-consciously. "If that's true, I'm really not going to dance."

"It's okay, baby girl. Just let yourself go with the music and follow my lead. Don't worry about who's looking at you. It's not about them. Dancing is liberating, so do it like nobody's watching," Stone said as he did some fancy footwork.

Like he'd told her to, Vintage followed his lead. After a few minutes, she had the basic moves, but she was stiff as a board. Stone put his hand on the small of her back.

"Arch your back a little and move your hips," he instructed as his hips dropped to her hips.

An electric shock felt like it had ignited every sensation between her thighs. As her womanhood tingled, she squeezed her thighs together, making her look even stiffer than before.

Stone let out a laugh. "Either you really can't dance, or you need another drink to let loose."

"I'm sorry." Vintage shook her head. "I told you I can't dance."

"Yes, you can. You're just overthinking things again."

Vintage shook her head feeling a little frustrated. She was really turned on and the alcohol was making it hard to be so close to him. Her body was defying all the logic in her mind and that was why she couldn't let herself go in the moment. She was afraid of what she'd end up doing if he ignited that flame that she'd always douse out.

"It's only dancing, baby. It's not that serious." With his hand on the small of her back again, he led the dance and she followed, letting her hips move that time. "There you go," he nodded with a satisfied grin on his face. "You got it."

Soon, Vintage was in the groove. Once again, Stone was right. She forgot that anybody was around them and just let her body go with the flow of the music. Sweat beaded on her forehead as they danced for hours straight. When a slower song came on Stone put his arms around her waist her close. It was sad that she was in her twenties and had never slow danced with a man before.

Laying her head on his shoulder, she wrapped her arms around his neck and closed her eyes. Damn, he smelled like heaven was on his flesh. Taking in a deep whiff, Vintage felt like her head was spinning. She'd never felt anything like that in her life. This time instead of running away from it, she was going to dive in head

first.

Chapter 7

Almost two months had passed since Sage's accident, and she was getting back to herself again. Vintage had talked her into talking to a therapist and had also had a few sessions with her. As far as seeing her on her own, she'd convinced herself that she was just too busy. The truth of the matter was, Stone seemed to be the one who was helping her cope, and she was just fine with that.

"So, are you and Stone an official couple yet?" Sage asked when she sat down at the table for breakfast.

"Well, good morning to you too," Vintage told her with a laugh.

"Good morning, but answer my question, ma'am." Sage was smiling, and to Vintage that was a good sight to see.

"Are you and Jose an official couple yet?" Vintage teased as she ate a forkful of cheese eggs.

"No, but he's definitely trying." Rolling her eyes, Sage took a bite of bacon.

"Give the man a chance. He really likes you," Vintage pointed out.

"Did I not tell you what he does for a living?" Sage countered.

"Well, you can possibly change his life. Give him a legal job. MS could use a handsome, Spanish realtor."

"He'd think I was crazy if I mentioned him getting a nine to five." Sage shook her head.

"So, how do you feel about going back to school?" Vintage knew that it was Sage's first day back on campus and her nerves were shot about it. There were still no clues as to who tried to kill her.

"I'm ready, but I don't know. What if...?"

"You'll have Jake with you." He was the guy Vintage had hired to keep a watchful eye on Sage.

"I guess that makes me feel better. At first, I thought of just finishing my degree online, but it's time for finals. I can't stop living. I won't."

"There you go." Vintage smiled. "I'm glad you're getting better, sis."

"Me too, because I thought I'd be looking like shit forever. I'm finally starting to look normal now that I don't look like the elephant man." She laughed, but Vintage didn't.

Sage still had a slight limp and wore a brace on her leg, but she was a champ at physical therapy. She'd been reassured that she'd eventually get one hundred percent usage of her leg. That was good news and seemed to lift her spirits.

"A'ight, Vin, I'm out."

"A'ight, be safe."

Sage headed outside just as Jake pulled up in the Black Suburban that was designated to drive her around in. Vintage couldn't help but worry about her. Trying to clear her head and think positively, she realized that she hadn't been to the shop in a while. Maybe it was time for her to go check up on things.

It was as if she had a sixth sense because as soon as the thought crossed her mind, her phone rang.

"Hello?"

"Vintage, it's Kellie. You have to come to the store now. It's on fire!" she screamed frantically into the phone.

"It's what?" Had she heard her right? Why the hell was her store on fire?

"On fire..."

"I heard you! Shit!" What could possibly happen next? Vintage didn't even want to know. "I'm on my way. Where are you? What happened?"

"I'm outside, when I got here just now to open the boutique, I saw the flames. Somebody must've seen it too and had already called the fire department. The firetruck was literally pulling up behind me, but I have no idea what happened to cause the fire," Kellie explained in tears.

Thank God nobody was hurt, but what could have caused it? The boutique had just been rewired a year ago.

In less than twenty minutes, Vintage pulled up in front of the boutique jumping out of the car before she could even stop good. She ran over to Kellie who was shaking her head with tears still streaming down her face.

"I wonder what could have possibly happened?" Kellie shook her head. "Thankfully nobody was in there."

"That I am thankful for too." However, the damage and merchandise Vintage had lost had crossed her mind to. It was a good thing she had insurance, but her mother's dream had gone up in the flames.

Making her way over to one of the firefighters, Vintage had so many questions. Hopefully, somebody could answer them. "Do you know what happened here?"

A tall, built dark-skinned dude turned around. "I'm Captain Lewis, and may I ask who you are?"

"Yes, I'm Vintage Saldana, the owner."

With a nod, he wiped sweat from his forehead with a handkerchief. "The strong smell of accelerant lets us know that fire was no accident. It was an act of arson. Do you have any enemies that you know of, Miss Saldana?"

It was as if she couldn't even hear anything else. The chaos around her was now silent as something donned on her. Somebody was out to get her, and Joshua crossed her mind immediately. He'd been quiet because he was planning the ultimate act of revenge. He knew that the boutique meant the world to her.

"Miss Saldana," Captain Lewis called out in an attempt to get her attention.

"Oh, I'm sorry. I was just... thinking. Uh, I don't have any enemies per se, but I had an issue not too long ago with my ex. He may still be harboring ill feelings towards me, but I never thought he'd take it this far," she admitted.

"You can share who this disgruntled ex is with Officer Crews over there." He pointed at a tanned white dude with blonde hair and blue eyes. Dressed in the standard blue uniform, he was standing there assessing the scene.

Making her way over to him, Vintage introduced herself and gave the officer her statement. "His name is

Joshua Anderson," she told him after giving a short rundown of their volatile break-up and the private video he'd shared of her on social media. It had been deleted so she didn't have the proof, but he was somebody to look into. Who else would set the boutique on fire and why?

Thinking about the fact that she now had to file an insurance claim, Vintage was pissed all over again. Who was hell-bent on destroying her and what she held dear? Not knowing was driving her crazy.

"Do you know his address?" The officer asked.

"Actually, I don't know where he's living right now." Damn, if only she'd found that Burberry shirt, she'd have his address.

"No worries. We will find out," the officer assured her. "If it's anything else you can think of, give me a call at the station. It's a possibility that it isn't him. Right now, there are no witnesses, so we'd have to have some way of connecting him to the crime if he's busy."

"Okay, thank you, and I will." Shaking her head, Vintage stared into the boutique's busted windows. Everything was wet, burned or covered in soot.

Feeling defeated, she decided to go home and deal with all of that later. On the way, she called Stone to tell him what was going on. She'd decided not to call her sister since she didn't want to ruin her first day back to school with bad news. It would probably be an omen to her that she should've stayed home.

"Vintage, what's up?" Stone asked sounding glad to hear from her.

"I know it's early, and I'm sorry for calling…"

"What's wrong?"

"Somebody set the boutique on fire," she simply told him.

"Oh… my… wow… Do you know who did it?" he asked sounding concerned, but his question was weird to her. He should've been asking if she was okay.

"No, but I told the police about my situation with Joshua. They are going to look into it, but it'll be hard to prove. We're hoping the surveillance from across the street caught something since the fire damaged all of my camera equipment." Vintage sighed heavily. "I'm just so frustrated at this point, Stone. It's one thing after another. We don't even know who did that shit to Sage."

"Calm down. I'm going to take you out to lunch, and I'm going to take the rest of the day off. I have to make sure that my woman is okay."

"Your woman? Is that what I am to you?" The grin on Vintage's face was a contrast to how she was feeling just a few minutes ago.

"Yes, although I know you're not ready for that, that's how I see you. I want to be with you and hopefully, eventually, you'll feel the same way. For the time being, I just want to be here for you in any way I can. Is that okay with you?" His voice was like a sweet melody in her ear.

"It's more than okay with me." Vintage was about to thank him, but she caught herself. That man had to be too good to be true, but she was convinced herself to enjoy it while it lasted.

"Good, I'll see you in a few hours. Until then, try not to worry. Okay."

"Okay," she agreed not knowing if she'd be able to do that.

* * *

After two weeks of wondering, Vintage finally had some answers about the fire at the boutique. Surveillance from the bank across the street showed a woman with long, dark hair pouring gasoline all over the storefront. Her face wasn't clear, but Vintage knew exactly who she was.

"That's Janelle," she told the detective who had played the surveillance video for her. Vintage hadn't even thought about her. "I fired her over six months ago. She was my assistant manager. I caught her stealing money."

"Disgruntled ex-employee instead of ex-boyfriend, huh?"

They hadn't found anything on Joshua of course, so Vintage was relieved to know that he was over it and moving on with his life. Knowing that Janelle had been the one to set the boutique on fire, she wondered if she was the one who had run Sage off the road too. Besides, Sage was the one who had figured out what she was doing.

"Can you see if she's connected to what happened to my sister?" Vintage asked anxiously wanting to put everything that had been happening behind her.

"Yes, we'll work on the warrant for her arrest. I'm sure you have her information on hand. That will make it easier to find her in case she has no criminal record. I assume you didn't report her for her theft."

"No, I didn't. I just fired her. Other than that, she was cool, and I didn't want to ruin her life. I regret that now."

Vintage left the police station relieved to know that Janelle was going to pay for what she had done. She'd given them her last known address hoping that she still lived there. A nagging feeling told her to pull up on Janelle herself, but she decided to let the law handle her.

She'd hate to get caught up in something that could really ruin her life.

Yet, and still, there was a burning desire inside of her to take a can of gasoline and set that bitch's house on fire. Then she'd know how it felt to watch something that was important to her go up in flames. She didn't know that Janelle was still bitter about her firing her. Now she did.

People kept on underestimating Vintage because they must've felt like she was soft, and they could get away with it. If she'd found out that Janelle had set the boutique on fire before the police saw that video, she would've taken matters into her own hands.

* * *

Over the next few days, Vintage called constantly to see if Janelle had been arrested.

"No one contacted you?" the woman asked as she typed vigorously.

"No, I mean, I wouldn't be calling if someone did."

Vintage didn't mean to come off as a smart ass, but that

was clearly a dumb question.

"I'm sorry Miss Saldana. One of the detectives on the

case was supposed to contact you directly. It turns out

that the suspect no longer resides at the address that was

given. At this point it's a matter of finding her and

bringing her in," she explained.

Not really knowing of anyone that Janelle knew,

Vintage didn't have any information to offer. The only

person she'd met was a boyfriend of hers named Carlos.

She didn't even know his last name, and they probably

weren't together anymore.

The thought of Janelle taking her revenge to the next

level crossed her mind. If they didn't catch her, Vintage,

Sage and whoever was close to them could possibly be in

danger. Not once did she ever think Janelle would be

capable of such craziness. She'd hired her because she

seemed so professional and well put together. That was

probably the con-artist in her. Obviously, the chick was beyond crazy.

"Well, until she is caught, I guess I'm on my own. If something happens, and I defend myself, I have the right to do that."

"You do," she confirmed.

"I'm sorry, but what did you say your name was again?"

"Amanda Reed."

"Thank you, Amanda."

Ending the call, Vintage didn't bother to speak to any of the detectives since they didn't bother filling her in on Janelle's arrest. Instead, she went upstairs and retrieved her 9 mm from a safe in her bedroom's closet. Making sure that it was loaded, she promised herself that she'd never leave home without it.

Chapter 8

Sage's limp wasn't as noticeable as before, and her beauty was as radiant as ever. Except for some slight swelling from her facial reconstructive surgery, there were no other signs that anything had ever happened to her. The thought burned Dayna up as she watched Sage make her way across campus. Cutting her brake line and running her off the road that day hadn't resulted in her death like she'd wanted it to. Now it was on to plan B.

"Next time, you gon' die, bitch." As she pulled off from the curb, she thought of all the things that had pushed her to the point of no return.

Sage was the "It Girl" on Spelman's campus. On the other hand, Dayna was the exact opposite. Socially awkward and not that attractive physically, she'd always felt rejected. With light, brown skin, and shoulder-length hair, her facial features were quite mousy. Standing at 5'10, she was lanky, clumsy and not very lady like.

She envied Sage's natural ability to be confident and graceful. Her poise alone made others notice and gravitate to her. Once in Biology class during their freshman year, Dayna was assigned to be Sage's lab partner. Sage made Dayna feel like she was beneath her, but she tried her best to ignore it. One day, Sage took things way too far.

While Sage was putting a sample under the microscope for them to look at, Dayna accidentally knocked the petri dish over that had the microorganisms they had to culture in it. It crashed onto the floor and broke into pieces. Sage looked at Dayna like she was crazy.

"Can you ever do something without messing it up? Those long ass arms of yours are always knocking something over. You can't even walk without tripping over your own two feet. Now, go get us another petri dish please, after you clean that shit up," Sage chastised her.

"I... I didn't mean to..."

Sage cut her off. "I... I... don't care."

134

Dayna always stuttered uncontrollably when she was nervous or embarrassed. Tears burned her eyes as she cleaned her mess up while everyone laughed. After getting another petri dish and what else they needed, Dayna tried to not let what Sage said bother her. All she wanted was to finally be accepted by her peers. Maybe she needed to work on being less... weird. Not into the latest fashions, her clothes weren't fashionable, and Sage gave her hell over that next.

"Where the hell do you get your clothes from?" she asked all loud, so everybody could hear her.

"Different places," Dayna simply answered in a soft voice.

"Different places like thrift shops?" Sage joked and everybody in earshot laughed on cue. They all wanted to be a part of her clique, so it was a given. To Dayna, college was no different than high school.

"What's wrong with shopping at thrift shops?" Dayna shrugged as she asked.

"Everything is wrong with wearing something that's been on somebody's else's ass. You need a make-over for real. You'll never get a man looking like that."

"Who said I wanted a man?" Dayna countered.

"Oh, so you're a lesbian then," Sage joked, and the laughter was even louder.

"No... I'm..." Looking around the room, Dayna could feel her head start to pound. Her blood boiled within her veins, and steam literally came from her ears. She was so upset that she actually stormed out of the class.

After that day, she avoided Sage. She even dropped the Biology class. Yet and still, the sight of Sage's face infuriated her. At first, she was attracted to her. Yeah, she was a lesbian, but that wasn't something that Sage should've teased her about. Now everybody was saying that she was gay like it was a bad thing. She'd recently embraced her sexuality but had lost her virginity to her high school boyfriend. She hadn't pursued a woman at that point, because at first, she wanted to be with Sage.

Once she embarrassed her, she started to really hate her. She hadn't hated someone so much in her life.

The straw that broke the camel's back had happened about a month before Dayna cut Sage's brake line. To her dismay, she ended up having the same Economics class as Sage. When Dayna spotted Sage sitting there in the front of the class, she knew that things would go left quickly. Over the years, Sage had bullied her whenever she saw her and made her life a living hell.

When Sage spotted Dayna, a sly grin spread across her face. "Dayna, it's been a while. I thought you finally dropped out."

Dayna didn't even react. She simply sat down at her desk and prayed for the class to end soon. She wanted to drop it, but she couldn't let Sage continue to have that control over here. Dayna had finally met a woman that she really cared about named Chantal. They met outside of class, and when Sage spotted them, she giggled with her little crew of followers behind her.

"Oh, so you do eat pussy," Sage let out when she caught them hugged up in the hallway.

"Fuck you, Sage," Dayna seethed angrily.

"I'm just saying. I don't see anything wrong with you liking chicks, but... I just don't understand what she sees in you. You must got some real pussy eating skills. Is that what it is?" she asked Chantal.

Chantal looked at Sage and then focused on Dayna. Her face had turned beet red, she was so angry. "Calm down, baby," Chantal tried to soothe her, but Dayna was beyond mad.

Sage walked off with her puppets and they all laughed and joked on the way. Later on, when Dayna and Chantal walked outside to the parking lot, they were still lingering around.

"Damn, you got a nice whip though. Maybe that's what your girl likes," Sage continued with her antics.

At the time her Charger was white, but she ended up getting a paint job a week later. That was to throw Sage off if she spotted her the night she put her plan into motion. Cutting her brake line wasn't enough. She had to have the satisfaction of watching her run off the road. That was going to make it all worthwhile because what she walked in on later that week turned her hate for Sage into something way more dangerous.

Chantal had just moved in with Dayna, and she was so in love with her. With flawless, milk chocolate skin, Chantal was a petite, but shapely. At 5'2, she was the cutest thing Dayna had ever seen. She didn't hold a candle to Sage though. As much as she made Dayna want to hurt her, she still desired her just as much.

After her last class of the day, Dayna went to her job at Wendy's at four o' clock. Her shift usually ended at eleven, but she had told Chantal that she had to work late since it was the weekend. Normally she would've got home after one on a Friday, but she ended up being able to leave early. She wanted to surprise her girl, so she didn't call her at twelve when she was on the way.

The Wendy's she worked at was less than ten minutes away, and all Dayna could think about was tasting Chantal. She'd finally found someone who loved and accepted her for who she was on the inside. They'd been together for almost a year, and she was really falling deeply in love with her.

When she got home, she rushed to her bedroom, undressing on the way. Chantal had literally moved in with her, so she knew she'd be waiting. She was home early and hoped Chantal would be happy to see her. Dayna pushed the door open and the sound of low moans greeted her ears. Turning on the light, Dayna expected to find someone in the bed with Chantal, but she was pleasuring herself.

With a smile on her face, Dayna made her way over to her lady ready to replace her fingers with her tongue. Chantal looked up at her with a startled look on her face. She scurried to pick up the phone that was propped up for her to watch what Dayna assumed was some porn. Dayna grabbed the phone to see what her girl was looking at.

"Dayna, stop! Give me my phone back!" Chantal demanded in a panic. Getting up from the bed butt naked, she jumped in an attempt to grab her phone as Dayna held it up out of her reach.

"Why? What the fuck was you doing?" Walking away from her with long strides, Dayna was able to see exactly who had Chantal turned on.

Staring back at her was a sexy image of Sage on her Instagram page. So, she was into Sage? The thought infuriated Dayna, and she tossed Chantal's phone against the wall.

"Why did you do that?" Chantal screamed as she attempted to pick her broken phone up from the floor.

"So, you want her?" Dayna screamed in a rage. "You want the bitch who bullies me right in front of you? That's who the fuck you want?"

"No... babe, I... she's just a fantasy," Chantal admitted and before she could stand up, Dayna kicked her right in the face.

"A fantasy? A fuckin' fantasy!" Dayna snapped.

Chantal grabbed her cheek as Dayna continued to physically assault her. With each punch and kick, Chantal cried out, balling into the fetal position. It wasn't like Dayna to be physically violent, but she was harboring years of being bullied and pushed around. Now it was time for her to turn the tables. She knew that if she wanted to be with Chantal, she had to get rid of that bitch Sage.

After Dayna came to her senses, she calmed down. Chantal's face was bloody as she moaned, letting the tears fall. "I'm so sorry, baby," she moaned in agony. "I never meant to hurt you. Please, don't hit me anymore"

Her voice was low and pleading as Dayna finally ended her assault. Breathing hard, Dayna didn't know what to do next. Her instinct was to apologize to Chantal, but she couldn't say anything to her. It broke her heart to know that she'd hurt the woman that she loved.

"Shit, Chan, I... I'm... s... so s...sorry baby. I..." Helping her up from the floor, Dayna walked her into the bathroom to clean her face up.

Chantal ended up forgiving her after she vowed to never put her hand on her again. She did have something she needed her to do to assure that though. "I want you to help me get rid of her."

"Who?" Chantal asked as they sat down at Starbucks with their usual double mochas with whipped cream.

"Sage," Dayna simply stated as if Chantal should have known.

"Get rid of her how?" Chantal's face fell as she considered what her girlfriend was asking of her.

"For good. Don't play dumb. I can't let her live if we're going to be together," Dayna explained.

"What do you mean, Dayna. It's no way we can do that. She's no threat to us. It's not like it's something going on between me and her," Chantal protested.

"That doesn't matter. You can say what you want, but I know you're attracted to her. You said she's your fantasy. That means she has to go because she will always be a temptation to you."

"Dayna, you're overreacting."

"I'm not overreacting, Chantal and if you don't help me... I'll just have to get rid of you too."

Dayna didn't know if it was fear or love that made Chantal help her cut Sage's brake line that night she was parked in front of Jose's house. They'd followed her and made sure they stayed a few feet away, so Sage wouldn't know. After that, they camped out and waited for her to leave to finish the job.

Months later, and Dayna was pissed that her first attempt at taking Sage's life hadn't worked. Now she had a second chance. The Morehouse Kappa fraternity was throwing a party that night at their off-campus frat house. More than likely, Sage was going since it would be the last big party of the semester. That was where she'd end their feud once and for all. She just hoped Sage would show up.

Chapter 9

"It's no way I'm going to a party tonight, Danie. I ain't even in the mood," Sage complained.

Danielle's boyfriend Tyrell was a Kappa and a senior at Morehouse, so he would definitely be there.

"I can't even dance, and you know I be tearing it up. I got a reputation to uphold." Sage rolled her eyes as if Danielle could see her over the phone.

"So, what. You haven't been out in months girl. You're recovering really fast, so why not have some fun? As far as dancing goes, you'll be okay just moving to the beat. You ain't gotta do all that twerking and shit." Danielle laughed trying to lighten her friend's mood. She'd been so down since the accident, and she wanted to get her out of the house to cheer her up.

"I'm not going, but I hope you have fun," Sage said with her mind made up.

"You're gonna get dressed. I'm not taking no for an answer. I'll be there to pick you at about ten o' clock." Danielle hung up the phone after that letting Sage know that what she'd said was final.

If she wasn't dressed when she got there, Danielle was going to dress her herself. Then she was going to drag her ass to her car and put her in the passenger seat. It was that simple because she was tired of watching Sage wallow in her self-pity. Most days she was in good spirits, but on some days, she seemed withdrawn and depressed. That wasn't like her social butterfly of a friend, so Danielle wanted to help her spread her wings again.

To Danielle's pleasant surprise, Sage was dressed and ready to go when she got there. "So, what brought on the change of heart? I thought I was going to have to make your ass go."

"Vintage said the same thing you did and actually picked my outfit out. You two are a trip." Sage laughed and followed Danielle to her car.

"Vin's my homey, for real." Danielle laughed too. When they were in the car, she decided to ask Sage about Jose. She hadn't mentioned him lately.

"So, what's up with you and Jose? You haven't said anything about him in a while."

"It's nothing to say really. He's okay, but I haven't talked to him in a week or two. It's just too much pressure. He wants a relationship and..."

"And what? What's the problem? He seems like a good dude who's really into you."

"I don't want a drug dealer, Dani."

"You don't want nobody, period."

That shut Sage up because it was true. She knew that Jose liked her. Plenty of men claimed to like her, but that wasn't enough obviously. Clearly, Sage needed a man to really pull out all the stops if he wanted her. So far, not one man that she'd dated or slept with had done enough to capture and hold her attention for too long.

"You might be right about that. I just... I don't know. I just lose interest after a while. I can't help it."

"Sage, who do you think you're fooling? I know you, bih. One thing I know is that you will find something fucked up about a man to lose interest. You do it on purpose, and it's definitely something you can help. You have to learn to accept someone's flaws and all."

"I don't do flaws, ma'am. I like 'em when I don't know 'em. Point blank period. Time I get to know a dude, anything I may have felt just disappears."

"You got some real issues." Danielle shook her head, dropping the subject. She knew that Sage wasn't easy to get through to, so she just gave up. She hoped a real love would find her best friend one day and hold her hostage.

* * *

About an hour had gone by, and Sage was starting to enjoy herself. She was feeling the music, and the drinks were abundant. Not wanting to drink too much while on pain meds, she kept it light. With a Corona in hand, she looked up and noticed that Bryan was heading her way. A part of her wanted to confront him, but the other part didn't want to deal with him.

"I ain't have shit to do wit' what happened to you," he started as he sat down beside her on the sofa, "and I'm glad you're okay."

"Thanks, and I know," Sage admitted with a huff. "You did threaten me though... so..."

"I was just feeling some type of way 'cause you don't want me. To be for real about it, I was starting to catch feelings for you. I ain't know how to handle it, but I ain't mean none of that shit I said. I would never do anything to hurt you," Bryan explained sincerely.

By that time, the place was packed with partiers wall to wall. It was hard to walk through the place, so Sage had found her a seat and stuck with it. Danielle was in a corner hugged up with her boo, and she didn't want to interfere.

"I appreciate that Bryan. I just don't know who to look out for anymore. My sister even hired security for me but allowed me to have some space tonight. It's crazy having to look over your shoulder all the time, you know?" Sage's eyes burned with tears, but she willed them away not wanting to look weak in front of him.

"The cops said that the person who did that to you drives a black Charger. I think I saw a black Charger outside." Bryan looked around. "I don't know who's driving it though."

"For real?" Sage asked feeling a chill travel over her.

"Uh huh... that's why I came over to talk to you. You should let me take you home, just in case something..."

Sage laughed in his face. "You tried it, but I'm good." In her mind, he was just trying to get her in bed again. What a desperate attempt to get with her. Why did he think she'd fall for that shit?

"Oh, so you think I'm tryin' to get some?"

"Are you?"

He shook his head. "No, I'm not. I'm really being serious right now."

"Okay, Bryan. Thanks, but no thanks. I came here with Dani, and I'm leaving with her." With that said, Sage stood and walked over in Danielle's direction. A queasy feeling came over her, and she wondered if the person who'd tried to kill her was around for real.

Before she could even get to where Danielle was, someone in a black hoodie walked toward her with their head down. The person was tall and thin, but she couldn't see their face. As they approached, Sage was nudged out of the way by someone. Not realizing what had happened right away, she watched as the girl who had pushed her collapsed to the floor shaking as if she was having a seizure.

The hooded figure just walked off as Sage called out after them. *What just happened*, she wondered. "Hey... hold up... Wait!" She followed the person but couldn't really keep up due to her still sore leg.

When the person in the hoodie started to run, Sage made her way over to the front door and watched as they got behind the wheel of a Black Charger and drove off.

"She's dying!" Sage heard someone yell out. Knowing that the girl was probably in that position because of her, Sage rushed back inside to see what was going on.

Kneeling over her, she realized that it was Chantal, who was Dayna's girlfriend. Then she remembered that Dayna drove a white Charger. Now it was black. It occurred to her that Dayna was who was wearing the black hoodie.

Chantal was foaming at the mouth and everything, but she tried to speak. "Day... na... did this... and sh... she... ran... you off the road. She... wants... to kill... to kill... you..." she gurgled, struggling to take a breath.

That was when Sage noticed a syringe on the floor beside Chantal. The wail of a siren in the distance let her know that an ambulance was on the way. Chantal's eyes rolled back in her head as her body convulsed again. With tears in her eyes, Sage recalled how she'd teased and taunted Dayna to no end. How could she have been so cold and cruel to someone? Now that shit was coming back to haunt her full force. Still, that was no reason for Dayna to want to kill her. If anything, she should've come to her like a real woman.

The paramedics rushed inside interrupting Sage's thoughts of regret. "Somebody stuck her with something. The syringe is right there," Sage told them quickly.

"Did you see who it was?" one of the EMTs asked.

Sage shook her head. "No," she told them, although she did.

Wanting to get her own street justice, she decided to keep the fact that the person who'd tried to kill her and had possibly killed Chantal was named Dayna Greene.

* * *

Over breakfast the next morning, Sage blurted out to Vintage, "I know who tried to kill me."

"Was it, Janelle?" Vintage's wide eyes caught hers.

"No," Sage looked away, feeling like maybe she had really pushed Dayna that far. Yet and still, she was angry as hell. "It was this chick named Dayna. She goes to Spelman. I uh... over the years... I haven't really been that nice to her. You can say that I probably pushed her enough to make her hate me."

"What? How do you know it was her, and why would you be so cruel, Sage? You weren't raised that way at all." Vintage shook her head at her sister.

"I know it was her because at the party last night, she attempted to kill me again. Her girlfriend ended up pushing me out of the way, and she got poked with the syringe instead."

"Syringe?" Vintage stared at Sage. "Hold up… She tried to stick you with a syringe?"

"Yeah, but her girlfriend Chantal must've known about her plan because she pushed me out of the way just in time. After that, Dayna rushed off, and I watched her get in a black Charger."

"Are you going to tell the police?" Vintage dropped her fork on the plate in front of her.

"No."

"Why not? I'm going to tell them then." Vintage knew that she already had Janelle to handle. Dealing with that Dayna chick threatening her sister's life was going to be a battle too.

"Just like you have been as of lately, I stay strapped too. Now I know who to shoot," Sage stated before taking a sip of coffee.

"Sage, do you even know how to shoot that gun?" Vintage may have been more on the quiet side, but she was consistent with going to target practice.

"No, not really... but I figured if I aim and pull the trigger..."

"Nope, wrong answer." Vintage shook her head. "We're going to target practice tomorrow."

"Okay," Sage agreed before digging into her breakfast.

"So, that girl died?" Vintage asked.

"Yeah, I don't know what was in that syringe, but I'm sure it'll all come out after they test it."

Vintage shook her head. "Shit's been really crazy lately. I'm glad you're done with your classes now."

"Uh, I do have one more final to take next week, Vin. Don't worry. I got security on it, remember? Besides, that bitch just killed her girlfriend, so I doubt she'll be on campus. She knows I saw her. She'll think I told the cops."

"I don't know why you won't."

"Because I'll be looked at as the bad guy. That bitch will plead insanity and get off. I'll be the reason she suffers from PTSD and all types of shit. It'll all be my fault. Think about it. Bullying is like the number one thing not to do right now. It won't matter that she tried to kill me. Some people will justify that shit."

"I seriously doubt that, Sage. Murder is murder, and there's no way she can get away with killing her girlfriend and trying to kill you. She's a threat to society."

"Right," Sage agreed, "but, what if she does get away with it? I can't let that happen."

"Wow, so what are you going to do, murder the girl?"

Sage shrugged. "I ain't no killer but don't push me." Getting up from the table, she put her empty plate in the dishwasher. "I'm going out with Jose later," Sage threw over her shoulder and walked toward the stairs. Her limp was less and less noticeable every day, but she continued her physical therapy.

The thought of her sister genuinely liking somebody made Vintage smile, but she was worried about Sage. What if that chick finally did the deed? She was hell-bent on killing her. Vintage put her plate in the dishwasher and headed up to her room.

She had to look for that Dayna bitch on social media. There was no way she couldn't find out what she looked like. It wasn't just out of curiosity but out of necessity. At that point, she'd be looking out for her too. Dayna had a Facebook page, but no Instagram or Twitter. The only way that she knew it was the right person was because her profile stated that she was a student at Spelman.

Not that Dayna was ugly or anything, but she had a self-esteem problem. She was insecure and not really comfortable in her own skin. That was clear from her posts and the fact that she hardly ever posted any pictures. There was only her profile picture and a picture of who Vintage assumed was Chantal.

Now, Chantal was really cute. It was sad that she had lost her life over nothing but foolishness. Vintage shook her head, mourning for the girl she didn't know. She'd died way too soon and hadn't had the change to experience life. In a way, Vintage was angry at Sage for creating such a hostile situation. On the other hand, she felt that Dayna should've found a way to be stronger.

The sound of Vintage's phone ringing made her think about Stone. She'd been so preoccupied that she hadn't seen him in a while. They talked on a regular basis, but it was as if their relationship was at a standstill. Vintage looked down at her phone's screen and grinned when she saw that it was Stone calling. Not wanting to seem anxious, she let the phone ring a few more times.

"Hello?"

"Hey, babe."

"Hey, Stone. How are you?"

"Better now that I'm hearing your voice. It's been a while, and I can't help but feel like you're avoiding me."

"It's not that. I just got a lot going on right now and..."

"And that's no reason to neglect your man." His voice was sharp and stern.

It turned Vintage on in a way, but she played it off. "Huh?"

"You heard me. That hasn't changed just because you're afraid to feel something for me."

"Who said I'm afraid?"

"Actions speak much louder than words, Vintage."

"Well, fear has nothing to do with us. I fear for my sister's life, and I wonder if the cops will arrest Janelle before I have to take matters into my own hands. If you haven't figured it out yet, my life doesn't revolve around you. I have more pressing shit going on."

"And I want to be there for you, but you won't let me."

Frustrated, Vintage decided to just end the conversation. Stone didn't realize that she needed her space, therefore, she had to tell him. "Right now, I think it's best that I have my space. Don't call me. I'll call you."

"Wow, okay. I guess I have no other choice but to respect that."

"You're right, you don't."

Stone stared at the phone after she hung up not believing that their conversation had made such a turn for the worst.

Chapter 10

Vintage preoccupied herself with making sure that the insurance policy for the boutique was being taken care of. She also made sure that she kept her strap in her purse since they hadn't caught Janelle yet. Then there was the matter with that chick Dayna and Sage. The morning after literally putting Stone on the back burner, Vintage decided to take Sage to target practice.

"Damn, teach me how to do that Miss Tomb Raider Sharp Shooter," Sage joked as Vintage hit the heart, head and abdomen of her target.

"You're silly," Vintage laughed as Sage pointed her own weapon and aimed at the target as it dropped and moved closer to her.

Five straight shots rang out and Sage was glad her ears were covered because it was extremely loud. When the target paper moved down the line, she squinted realizing that she'd only hit the arm and torso. Those weren't really deadly shots and Sage was disappointed that she didn't know how to shoot as well as Vintage.

"You have to practice, Sage. Don't get discouraged." Vintage stood behind her sister and helped her with her stance. "You have to focus on what you want to shoot. You can't just start busting."

"What? You sounding all gangsta," Sage teased.

"Well, I'm not trying to, but it is what it is."

When Sage aimed that time, she closed her left eye and focused on a head shot. The first shot missed, but the second one tore right into the target's forehead like a bull's eye.

"Yes!" Sage screeched and aimed again. That time she penetrated the target's heart.

"See, it's easy," Vintage said behind her with a nod.

After another hour of shooting, they decided to head out and get something to eat.

"What do you have a taste for?" Vintage questioned Sage.

"I'm craving some sushi," Sage said thoughtfully.

"Okay, that sounds good, but how was your date with Jose?" There was a sly grin on Vintage's face as she asked.

"It was actually amazing. He took me out to dinner and then we took a helicopter ride. I mean, I like him, but his way of life isn't what I want to be involved in."

"That's understandable but..."

"Look, Vin, you have to deal with your up and down feelings for Stone, so let me deal with my own shit," Sage huffed.

"Wow, alright. Do you."

Vintage pulled up to the Benihana on Peachtree Rd. and paid for parking.

"You mad?" Sage asked trying to look all innocent.

"No," Vintage simply stated before getting out of the car.

"Yes, you are. I can tell," Sage spoke up as she stepped out of the car and closed the door.

"Do you want me to be mad?" Vintage spun around on her heels and stared at her sister. "I don't really have any energy to invest in being mad at you when I have Janelle and Dayna to worry about."

Sage looked down at her phone with a shocked look on he face. "Well, you don't have to worry about Dayna anymore. Turns out she shot herself right after the party. Her body was just found in her car. She's dead."

She showed Vintage the posts on Facebook and the news story about what happened to Dayna. There was no mention of Sage's bullying, so that was a relief to her. No one knew that Sage was really Dayna's target and not Chantal. It looked like a murder-suicide, but Vintage and Sage both knew better.

"Damn." Vintage shook her head. Her sister had dodged death twice. She wasn't happy that two other people were dead, but she was happy to still have Sage in her life. "I'm glad it's over, but I wonder what was in that syringe."

"Yeah, me too," Sage agreed, grabbing her sister's arm as they headed to the restaurant's entrance.

* * *

A few weeks later, it was revealed that pure hydrogen peroxide was in the syringe that Dayna had tried to stick Sage with. In the bloodstream, pure hydrogen peroxide would cause severe burning sensations as the compound destroyed every cell it touches. As it flowed along the bloodstream it would quickly turn into H_2O and O_2. Blood vessels would pop under the pressure, causing internal bleeding. Within seconds the victim would collapse and die from internal bleeding or organ failure. Sage could recall when they'd learned about that in Biology class.

That shit creeped Sage out, and she couldn't help but wonder if she'd be dead if Dayna had tried that method first.

"Who would do some shit like that to somebody?" Jose asked after she explained it to him.

They'd been spending a lot of time together lately, and Sage wasn't even bothered by it. She actually enjoyed his company, despite the lifestyle he lived.

"It's my fault, Jose. I... well, you can say that I bullied that girl so much, and she clearly already had some mental issues. I'm lucky to still be alive and believe me, I've learned my lesson the hard way."

He pulled her into his arms and kissed her forehead. "No matter what you did or said to her, she had no right to try to take your life. She had no right to kill her girlfriend. I understand your guilt, but you gotta forgive yourself, baby. You've been through enough."

Moving out of his grasp, Sage stood up and grabbed her shoes.

"Always running," Jose spat as he shook his head. "Why do you do that?"

"I'm not running. I just need to go."

"Why?" he pressed.

Sage shrugged her shoulders and sighed in frustration. "I just need to be alone right now, Jose."

"Why?"

"Is that the only word you know now? You can be so damn annoying," she huffed as she tied her sneakers up.

"And I won't even say what you can be, Sage!" Jose shook his head. "I'm just trying to understand you. I wear my heart on my sleeve, and you just keep on stomping on it."

"Because, as I told you before, I don't want to be in a relationship. Why do you keep pushing it?"

"Because I want you! Moments like this I wonder the hell why, but I do! Okay. Damn. What's stopping you from being with me?"

"You're a damn drug dealer, Jose. Add that to the fact that I just don't want a boyfriend. I love being single. I don't have to answer to anybody, and I don't have to worry about anybody hurting me. Not only that but if I don't catch feelings, I won't have to worry about losing somebody else that I love." There, it was out, and Sage felt better.

"Who said I'm a drug dealer?" Jose looked confused as hell.

"You did. You said you have an import/export business. You act all thuggish all the time and shit. What else would that mean?"

Jose chuckled, shaking his head at her. "I don't sell drugs, Sage. My father really does own an import/export business, and I work for him. Everything that we ship in and out is one hundred percent legal. I act the way I do because I'm a twenty-three-year-old man who was raised in the hip-hop culture. Stop reading more into it than it is. Everything ain't always what it seems."

"What? So, you really don't sell drugs?"

"No," he reiterated firmly.

"Damn, my bad. I guess I always think the worst."

"Yeah, you do. You were wrong about me, baby girl. Now does that change your mind about us?" His eyes were anxious as he stared down at her.

"Sort of, but not really. I still need to go for now, but... I won't keep running away."

By that time Jose was standing in front of her. She wrapped him in her arms for a nice, warm hug and then planted a soft kiss on his lips. "I can't promise you anything else," she added.

"All I want is a chance. That's it." Looking deeply into her eyes, his grip on her became tighter. He didn't want her to leave.

"I'll see you tomorrow, Jose," Sage confirmed.

"You promise?" His grip on her waist loosened.

"Yes, I promise."

Against his will, he let Sage go. Watching her leave, he wished she'd finally see that he was deeply in love with her. All he wanted to do was make her happy.

* * *

Vintage was sitting on the sofa binge-watching *Riverdale* on Netflix. Getting into the second season, she couldn't help but feel like life imitating art. What she'd been going through mirrored the tumultuous events of the characters down to the damn black hooded chick who had tried to kill Sage.

The sound of the doorbell made her heart pound. She wasn't expecting anybody, so she wondered if Janelle had finally decided to show up at her door. Vintage wondered if she'd be that bold because she was bold enough to set her boutique on fire. The police still hadn't found her, and Vintage was waiting for the confrontation that was sure to happen.

With her strap in hand, she walked over to the door and looked out of the peephole. Stone was standing there with a dozen white roses in his hand. Vintage's heart dropped. She placed the gun on the table near the door. Weeks had passed by, and she still hadn't called him. He'd been calling her, but she hadn't answered.

Not really wanting to deal with him and her emotional rollercoaster of feelings, she thought about ignoring him. The thought of sitting right back down on the sofa occurred to her, but after seeing Stone's face, she just couldn't do it. Reluctantly, she swung the door open.

"Hey Stone," she greeted him dryly.

"Well, it's nice to see that you're okay, stranger." He thrusted the roses toward her. "I got you these."

Vintage reached out and took the roses from him. "Thank you, but you should've called before you came."

"I did, but you didn't answer. I've been calling you for weeks. I need to know where we stand," he told her with a serious look on his face. "Do you still need your space?"

"Why're you pushing the issue? I don't recall making a commitment to you."

He cut her off. "This isn't about a commitment, Vintage. It's about common courtesy. We were dating on a regular, and you know that I have feelings for you. If you don't want to take things any further, just let me know. Just be straight up with me."

"I don't even know what I want right now, Stone. To be honest with you, I need to handle my business matters and everything else before I can even think about going any further with you. I don't want to hold you back. I'm just not ready, so do you. You're a good man, and I'm sure there's someone out there for you. Don't waste your time with me," she attempted to sway his feelings for her.

"I know there's someone for me, and it's you. It's nobody else. I'm willing to wait, Sage. My patience is so crazy right now because I know what I want." He stared down at her with such longing in his eyes.

"Thank you for the flowers, Stone, but... I really think you should leave."

"Just don't shut me out of your life. I'm fine with being your friend, Vintage. I want to be here for you. I do." His eyes were pleading.

"Okay, okay... I'll be in touch... for real this time."

Stone nodded before turning to leave. Vintage felt like shit for pushing him away, but she didn't know any other way to deal with how she was feeling. She was just afraid to get too close to him. A foreboding feeling told her that she wouldn't be able to control herself with him, and she wasn't ready to lose herself in love again.

* * *

"Danie!" Sage called out as she pulled up in her bestie's driveway. Danielle was checking her mailbox. Sage's twentieth birthday was approaching, and they were planning the festivities. She was so relieved that the shit with Dayna was over, but she was still dealing with her feelings of guilt. Not only that, but Janelle was still out there. She and Vintage had to stay on their P's and Q's.

"You ready to go see the venue?" Sage asked.

Danielle was looking down at the mail in her hand. "Nothing but junk. Yeah, girl." She got in the car with Sage. "What's going on with you boo?"

They hugged before Sage pulled off. "Just trying to keep my head on straight," Sage told her.

"I know. That shit that happened with old girl was crazy." She didn't even want to mention Dayna's name.

"Not just her. Jose is so adamant about us being together. He's so persistent, but in a good way." Sage continued. "Most dudes be on that crazy shit, but what he says is actually rational. Then he set me straight about what he does. I even did my research and he's telling the truth. He's not a drug dealer like I thought."

Danielle laughed. "So, you mean to tell me that you thought the man was a drug dealer because he said he worked for an import/export business. You are so paranoid."

"It's not that. It's just… that shit sounded like code for drug dealer to me." Sage laughed. "I'm glad to know he isn't a thug like that, although he got that thugged out swag."

"You like him." Danielle glanced over at Sage. "Stop fighting it."

"It's not that I'm fighting it. Shit, my feelings be fighting me. I don't know how to love a man since I lost my father. It hurts too bad to bond and then have it broken forever. Forever is so permanent, Dani. I don't want to have my heart broken again. I don't think I can take it. My heart isn't made of elastic… mine breaks."

"Your heart isn't any different from anybody else's. You're not unbreakable, but you can heal. That's a given. Look at you after all the shit you've been through. You do bounce back, Sage. Give yourself more credit. You're much stronger than you think." Danielle grabbed Sage's hand and squeezed reassuringly.

"But what if I go there with Jose and he hurts me.? It's going to be your fault, bih." They both laughed.

"You gotta take a chance, Sage. That's life."

"Yeah, yeah, but at the end of the day, I gotta be the one to pick up the pieces of my broken heart if shit goes left."

Danielle shook her head. "Nah, bestie, I'll be there to help you put it all together. You've always done that for me."

"And I always will," Sage confirmed knowing that the past few months had made her a different person. Bad karma wasn't something that she wanted to keep putting out there. Maybe her strings of broken hearts weren't helping. Maybe, just maybe, it was time for her to try something different.

* * *

"This shit is nice, but... it's too damn cold for a winter rooftop party, Sage."

They were in Buckhead at a building that rented out the rooftop for parties. It was December and the weather in Atlanta was windy and cold, especially downtown.

"I know it's going to be cold, but on my birthday, it will be fifty degrees that night. There are heaters strategically spaced. Believe me, this shit's going to be lit," Sage said excitedly.

"I mean, it's good to see you excited about something, but are you sure about this?" Danielle looked skeptical as hell about a party on the roof in the cold.

"Hell yeah, I'm sure. We only live once, right? We gon' turn this shit into a winter wonderland."

"Okay," Danielle agreed.

The fee was paid in full for the party and they headed to Danielle's car. She still couldn't understand why Sage wanted her party to be outside on a roof even if heaters were available. Danielle also knew that Sage was so popular that people would come party with her no matter what the circumstances were.

A woman was standing by the car with her back turned to them. Sage knew who it was right away. Instinctively, she reached in her purse and grabbed her gun. When the chick turned around, Sage had her weapon pointed.

"What the fuck are you doing here?" Sage asked Janelle before cocking her weapon.

"Just checkin' up on my old friend. Your birthday's coming up. Did you think I'd forget? Your birthday is exactly a month after mine," Janelle said with a smile.

"Girl, bye. You know ain't nobody fucking with you after the stunt you pulled. The cops are looking for you, you know?" Sage didn't even hesitate to keep her gun on her. "What the fuck do you want?"

"All I wanted to do was talk to you, Sage. I ain't mean to snap, but I lost everything after your sister fired me. I was desperate for revenge, but I'm over it now. I got some help, and I'm good now," she told Sage.

"Who the hell do you think you're fooling, Janelle? Definitely not me."

When Danielle pulled her phone out to call the police, Janelle showed her true colors. The gun that she had in her hand was visible. She aimed at Danielle. "Put the phone down bitch!"

Danielle dropped the phone, although Sage was pointing her gun at Janelle. She didn't want to chance getting shot.

"Good." Janelle sneered. "If you don't want your lil' follower to get shot, Sage, you'll put your gun down."

"Look around, Janelle. You don't think somebody will see this? We are out in the open in broad daylight. Somebody has called the cops by now. They're already after you."

"Put the gun down or that bitch's gon' get shot!" Janelle warned.

Sage put her gun on the ground. It was a good thing she had a small 22 in her bag too. She just had to find the right time to grab it without Danielle getting shot in the process.

"This is between me, you and Vintage, Janelle. Don't take it out on her." Sage put her hands up in an attempt to talk Janelle down.

"But she's close to you, so it makes her fair game." There was a smirk on Janelle's fast. "What do I have to lose, Sage? I lost my home, my man and my child."

"Is that my fault? You stole from me and my sister. You lost all of that because of you, not me. It's not fair to blame me or my sister for what you've gone through," Sage tried to reason with her but to no avail.

One shot rang out and Danielle fell to the ground. At that moment, Sage knew that she had to do something. Grabbing the 22 from her bag, she aimed and let a round off. The bullet hit Janelle right in the forehead and she was down.

"Danie," Sage kneeled next to her friend. The blood poured from her chest and her eyes were closed. "Danie!"

Sage pulled out her phone and called 911. "My friend has been shot. You have to get here fast. I had to shoot the person who shot her. Hurry!"

"What's your location?" the dispatcher asked.

Sage ratted off the address and put her phone down. Applying pressure to Danielle's wound, Sage closed her eyes and said a silent prayer. There was no way she could lose her best friend. Begging God to spare Danielle, the tears slid from her eyes.

"Just please let her survive this, God. Lord, if you don't want me to lose it, you have to save her. I can't take anything else." By that time the ambulance had arrived.

* * *

"Janelle is dead," the detective who had been on the arson case explained to Vintage and Sage at the police station.

Danielle had survived to Sage's relief. She was in stable condition. Thankfully, her best friend was okay. She was going to be okay, and that was a relief because she couldn't live with that guilt on her heart too.

Chapter 11

"Dani, can you hear me?" Sage asked, holding on to Danielle's hand as she rested in the hospital bed.

Danielle stirred and opened her eyes. "Yes, I can hear you. Did that bitch die?" Her voice was faint.

Sage nodded. "Yes, she did."

The heart monitor beeped and the IV drip with the pain medicine in it was sending feel good juice into Danielle's veins every few hours.

"Good," Danielle said before drifting off again.

Sage sat there for hours watching her friend's chest rise and fall as she slept. At that moment, she vowed to be a better person as hot tears spilled down her cheeks.

* * *

With all the evidence against Janelle, Sage wasn't charged with anything. Clearly, she had acted in self-defense. Yet and still, Sage was dealing with a lot. Dayna and Janelle's deaths along with Chantal's were taking a

181

toll on her. Due to that fact, she made an impromptu appointment to see her therapist.

"Miss Saldana, what brings you here today? We are not scheduled to see one another for another two weeks," Doctor Silva greeted her.

He was an older, dark-skinned man with close-cut salt and pepper hair and a tall, muscular build.

With a sigh, she sat down. "I have some things I need to get off my chest."

After she filled him in on the latest events, he simply nodded. "Guilt is a normal response to the trauma you've experienced. However, you must find a way to forgive yourself. You can't live with all that weighing on your heart and mind. It's only going to make your anxiety worse."

"I know, but I'm only human, Doc. I can't convince myself that my actions didn't cause everything. It was like a domino effect. Yeah, I know that Dayna had some issues and Janelle was dealing with some problems, but the things I did only added to it. I'm not a good person at all. As a matter of fact, I'm a horrible person. It's like... I don't know any other way to be. I don't do it for attention or anything like that. I'm just being myself. I have to admit that, I can do better. I'm going to do better. I love my sister, and I'd never want the things I do to affect her in a negative way. Then I had to see my friend lying in a hospital bed with a gunshot wound because of me. It could've been so much worse but thank God it wasn't." Sage wiped her tears away with a tissue that Doctor Silva had passed her.

"At least you are able to reflect instead of deflect."

She smiled through the tears. "I've been working on that. Instead of pretending that everything is okay, I'm starting to deal with the reality of things. I know that I'm not perfect, and that's okay. I don't have to be. Nobody has to be. It took a while for me to realize that."

"So, what now? What are your plans for bettering yourself?" He studied her over the top of his wire-rimmed glass.

Sage shrugged as she thought about. "I really don't know where to start. I guess I'll have to take it one day at a time. Instead of finding the bad in people, I'll look for the good. If I can't find anything good, that's fine. I don't have to point out everybody's flaws. I'm sure they already know all about them."

"Right," Dr. Silva agreed as he jotted some notes down in his notepad.

"And I'm going to work on my belief that I'm better than other people. I find myself competing with other women, even when I have no reason to. If they're not as attractive as me, or if they don't dress better than me, I have to speak on it. I'm working on that because everyone is different. If everybody was the same, this world would be a boring place. I'm accepting that it's okay for me not to be the prettiest or the best-dressed person in the room. I'm also accepting that if I am, it doesn't mean I have to make others feel bad about it. It's not worth it in the end. Everybody has feelings, and now I'm realizing that I do too."

"So, was there a time when you didn't feel anything?" Dr. Silva pondered with his hand under his chin.

"I guess you can say that I didn't want to feel anything. After my parents were killed, I decided to shut my feelings off. It was like a switch. That made life much easier for me, but I see that the feelings never went away. I just bottled them up and that was a big mistake. Now all my emotions are boiling over. It's so overwhelming. There I was thinking that I was controlling my feelings when I was just pretending to be numb. I didn't want to deal with anything if it didn't bring me pleasure. That shit definitely backfired on my ass," Sage explained as if Dr. Silva wasn't in the room.

He didn't mind being that he wanted her to express her feelings. She needed to purge all the negativity that she'd been experiencing since her parents' untimely deaths.

"Did hurting others cause you pleasure?" There was a contemplative look on Dr. Silva's face.

"Yes, it really did." Sage thought about it. "Maybe I was trying to fill some kind of void. I was empty and making others feel empty was my solution." She dabbed at her eyes. "Oh my god, I was really a bitch. I guess misery loves company, so I wanted to make other people feel miserable. I was hurt... so, I guess hurt people hurt people."

"And we have discussed that." Dr. Silva took his glasses off and leaned forward. "I think you're finally getting it, Sage."

"It took me almost losing my life three times, but I am." She was finally willing to take the blame for her own mistakes.

* * *

"What you got going on this weekend?" Jose asked Sage. They'd been exchanging small talk over the phone for the past ten minutes.

"Nothing, really."

To Jose, she sounded down. "You okay?" His voice was full of concern.

"I will be. Dani is home now. I'm just glad that she's okay. I've never had to... you know... *kill* somebody before. This shit is hard as hell. Then my birthday is coming up, and I don't even want a party now." The tears scorched her eyes, but she held them back. At that point, she felt all cried out.

"What do you want then?" All Jose wanted was a clue of how to make her smile. He just wanted to make her happy. Against his will, she'd touched his heart in a special way. As much as she defied their connection, he wasn't willing to let her go that easily.

"That's the hard part though. I really don't know. I guess, I just want to be surrounded by those I care about. That's a small crowd." Sage was used to being extravagant and going all out on her birthday. This time, she wanted something intimate and simple.

"I can handle that though. No worries. You're celebrating your birthday, baby girl. I'm gonna make sure of that."

"Aww, Jose, thank you." Sage was really touched.

"I care about you, Sage. You know that. Now, like I asked you a few minutes ago, what are your plans for this weekend."

"I guess we're going to do something together since you keep on asking." A wide smile decorated her face.

"I got plans for us, Sage. We can take over the world together on some power couple shit. For real." His voice was so stern and dominate that it made Sage feel something she knew was beyond anything she'd ever felt before.

"I'm scared, Jose," Sage admitted, allowing herself to be transparent for once. "I mean, I'll be twenty soon, and suddenly I feel so old. I'm still so young though. Like, am I ready to take a relationship to the next level? You have been persistent but in a good way. I don't want to keep running away from how I feel for you, but I don't want to fail at this. I just know I'm going to fail. I'll be a terrible girlfriend. My mouth is reckless, I don't feel like I should have to answer to anyone, and I don't know if one man can satisfy me. You sure you want to take that chance?"

188

"I know for a fact that I want to take that chance with you. It's no question. Let's just let it flow, baby. I can deal with your mouth, and you don't have to answer to me. You just will because of the mutual respect between us. As far as other men, I ain't worried. They ain't got nothing on me. I'm sure I'll have no problem keeping you satisfied in every way."

"Hmm... well... I guess we're going to see." Sage squeezed her eyes shut as she thought about what she was agreeing to. She'd never been in a real relationship before.

"Yes, baby. That's what I'm talkin' 'bout. So, I'll see you Friday at 'bout six. Pack a bag with a pair of comfy pajamas. You already sex as hell, so you ain't gotta try hard. I'm kidnapping you until Sunday. I want you all to myself the whole weekend."

That made Sage smile even harder. "Okay. I can't wait."

When she hung up, she realized that she didn't have one regret. After almost being killed three times, she realized that it was time to take a chance on love.

* * *

Jose's father owned a beautiful lake house on Lake Allatoona. He'd given his son the keys just for the occasion. It was a log cabin that was right there by the water. Although it was cool outside, it was early Fall, so it wasn't too cold. The temperature had dropped to sixty-one degrees after the sunset.

"My parents can't wait to meet you. Of course, they know all about you. I'm just waiting for you to let me know when you're ready," Jose told Sage as he grabbed her hand and led her inside the two-story log cabin.

"Wow, this is so gorgeous." Sage's breath caught as they stood in the foyer hand in hand. The cabin looked so much bigger on the inside. She was also trying to avoid the conversation about meeting Jose's parents.

A winding, mahogany staircase with a beautiful crystal chandelier hanging over it beckoned them. Jose walked toward the sitting room with Sage's hand still secured in his. The furniture was modern, but warm and inviting. The living room was decorated in brown and green earth tones. There was an old-fashioned fireplace that caught Sage's eye right away, giving the place that rustic charm.

"Just wait until you see the bedroom." Jose winked at Sage. "We'll save it for last though."

Jose walked off and lit the fireplace. "I told you to bring a cozy pair of pajamas because we're going to drink hot chocolate, eat some homemade soup my momma made and watch some scary movies."

"Homemade soup?" That sounded good as hell to Sage because her grandmother made the best homemade soup and chili. She also loved scary movies. "I haven't had homemade soup in so long. What's in it?"

"How about I heat some up while you get comfy. I'll meet you on the couch in front of the TV." His wide smile made her feel so relaxed.

"Okay," she agreed before sauntering off to take a quick shower. The cute little Hello Kitty onesie she'd packed up was perfect for cuddling in front of the fireplace and watching scary movies while indulging in hot-chocolate and soup. The sexy lingerie she would've normally have worn to seduce stayed in the drawer. This was something different.

The thought made Sage smile too. Never in her life had something so simple, meant so much. Maybe she had never really been impressed because other men she'd dealt tried too hard with the superficial shit. She had money and nice things already, so she only needed a man to touch her soul. That was something she didn't even know she needed until that very moment.

Per instructed, she headed to sit down in front of the TV. Jose came into the room with a tray for her. The delectable aroma coming from that bowl made her stomach growl. It looked more like a Brunswick Stew than a regular soup and tasted delicious. There were two sweet, cornbread muffins on the side. The hot chocolate had small marshmallows in it and whipped cream on top.

Sage felt like a little girl again as Jose sat down beside her with his tray. "I had to taste it. It's so good. Your mother's going to have to teach me to make this."

"And she will. I told you my parents can't wait to meet you." Jose smiled at me before he dug in.

"So, what are we watching?" Sage kept her eyes on him as he grabbed the remote to start the movie.

"I know that you like the classics. Friday the 13th is your favorite, but I picked a Nightmare on Elm Street because we are on a lake. I didn't know if you'd be freaked out tonight." He laughed.

"Freaked out? Shit... Jason doesn't scare me after what I've been through." She shrugged and sipped her hot chocolate. "I like Freddy though. He's funny as hell and he got swag."

"Swag?" Jose muttered with a chuckle before digging back into his food.

"Hell yeah, you'll see." Sage couldn't help but laugh too. "Look at his stance."

Once their bowls and mugs were empty, Jose put a blanket over them as they cuddled on the sofa.

"You smell so good?" he whispered in her ear.

"I thought you were watching the movie."

"I am, but I'm easily distracted by you. Besides, we've both seen it."

"So, what you wanna do then?" Although she asked, she already knew. His hardness had been poking her in the back for the past thirty minutes.

"You need to take this off now. I can't even get in that shit? What is it? I thought only babies and toddlers wear those?"

Sage laughed at Jose. "Obviously they make them for adults too, sir."

"I see, but when I said pajamas, I envisioned something that would make that pussy accessible. I wanted to play in it while we watch the movie, but nah, you had to wear this," he playfully complained.

By that time Sage was cracking up. One thing she loved about Jose was his sense of humor. Now that she knew he wasn't into the streets like that, she could actually relax with him. They'd known one another for less than a year, but to Sage, it was like she'd know him all her life.

"You're so silly, but why don't you take it off?" Suddenly her voice was serious as she turned to face him.

Their lips met, and their tongues connected in a sweet kiss. Before Sage knew it, she was out of that onesie. Jose positioned himself on top of her. His clothes were off fast too, and his warm lips were igniting a flame on her fevered skin.

"Mmmm..." she moaned as Jose's warm tongue traveled down between her thighs. "Ohhhh..."

As he licked, slurped and sucked, Sage closed her eyes, allowing the feeling to take over her being. Jose made love to her with his mouth, and as he blessed her anatomy with deep, warm tingles and multiple orgasms, she knew she wanted to return the favor.

After orgasm number two, she took it upon herself to assume the sixty-nine position. Jose was taken aback because she'd only performed oral sex on him once.

Losing control because Sage was taking him so deep down her throat, his knees buckled, and his toes curled. "Ohhh... myyyy... god... Sage..." He was out of breath and all.

Before he completely lost himself, he decided that he wanted to feel her. Assuming the position, he was now on top of her. He didn't even bother to grab a condom, and she didn't bring it up. They were a real couple and in both of their minds, it was whatever.

Consummating their commitment, Sage held on to Jose, grazing her fingernails up and down his back. Their bodies were in sync as if they had been made for each other.

"Damn, you fit me like a glove," he whispered in her ear.

Caressing his face, she stared up into his deep, dark brown eyes. The long lashes that hooded them added to her physical attraction to him. "Be careful with me," she mouthed.

"Always and forever, babe. I won't hurt you. That's my word."

The orgasmic rush took Sage's body hostage immediately, and as her eyes closed, Jose leaned over to kiss her eyelids.

Soon after, he was joining in her bliss and they held onto to one another as the flames from the fireplace danced seductively.

"God, I love you," Jose gasped.

He hadn't bothered to move and for the first time, Sage had allowed a moment in time to just happen. Not feelings one regret about it, she held on to him even tighter as he softened inside of her.

"I love you too," she confirmed before drifting off into a deep sleep.

At seven the next morning Sage woke up to the smell of breakfast cooking. She jumped out of the California King sized bed and headed to the master bath to take a shower. After brushing her teeth and pulling her hair back, she threw on a pair of tights and one of Jose's t-shirts.

Venturing down the stairs, the delicious smells coming from the kitchen made her mouth water. She was hungry after all the sex they'd had the night before. That was definitely a workout. Jose was smiling all hard when he took in the sight of her.

"You are too damn beautiful." Shaking his head, he gestured for her to sit down at the table.

"Thank you, handsome. I ain't never been waited on before."

"Well, it's a first time for everything, I guess." As he fixed their plates, Sage simply watched him.

Damn, he was so fine. The way his skin glowed in the light and those pretty ass eyes. His lips were the perfect size and his strong jawline defined his masculinity. Not only that, but he was looking like a whole buffet in his basketball shorts and a white tee.

"I was hungry as hell after my jog this morning," he explained after putting a plate in front of her.

After fixing his own plate, he sat down.

"So, you went jogging without me?" Sage glanced over at him before going in on the scrambled eggs, bacon, toast and grits.

"Well, I didn't think you could... plus you were sleeping so peacefully. I didn't want to bother you."

"This is good," she pointed out as he ate. "I need to exercise to get my leg back where it used to be. You had no problems last night when you were fucking me."

"I was making love to you." As he dug into his food, he licked his lips and stared into her eyes.

"Okay, well, either way, you weren't worried about my leg then." Sage rolled her eyes in annoyance.

"You really gon' act like that this early in the morning though? I'm sorry I didn't invite you to run with me. Next time, I will, okay. I didn't want to push you, but you're right. You did your thing last night, and I should've considered that."

"Thank you," she spat with a smile. "You put it down too." Not wanting the bring up the risks of her of being pregnant, Sage hoped her birth control pills worked. That one percent risk made her suddenly regret not asking him to use a condom.

"Shit," he chuckled. "I always put it down."

"Yeah, you do," she agreed as she cleaned her plate.

Once they were both done, Jose cleaned up and washed the dishes. Sage just sat there enjoying the fact that a man was doing more for her than having sex with her. It was clear that he really did care for her. Although she'd agreed to be in a relationship with him, she wondered if she was making the right decision.

"Love is a complicated thing, baby girl," Jose said as if she could read his mind. "You never know day to day where life might lead you, but when you really love somebody, you just know that they'll be there with you. They'll be willing to take the good with the bad. I ain't sayin' be stupid. I'm just sayin' that you gotta know that it's going to be ups and downs. Every day won't be perfect, but don't ever forget that you're so perfect for me." Cupping Sage's chin in his hand, he kissed her passionately.

Her heart pounded, and she shivered as his hands slipped under the shirt she was wearing. After he lifted it over her head, he took one of her already hardened nipples into his mouth.

"I'm so in love with you, Jose." Tears dripped from her eyes. "I didn't expect his."

"Sometimes when you least expect something it happens. This love between us is happening, so let it." His warm lips were on her flesh again.

Suddenly, Jose picked her up and carried her upstairs with her legs wrapped around his waist. After he laid her on the bed, he slowly undressed her. To her surprise, he didn't attempt to have sex. Instead, he came back to the bed with some kind of body oil in his hand. Then he rubbed her body down from head to toe.

The full body massage had her head swimming and her body felt like it was floating on a cloud. She'd been through so much severe physical pain that she thought my pain meds were all that could bring her relief. To her pleasant surprise what Jose was doing to her was just as good at easing it.

"Mmm... that feels so good, baby," she moaned with her eyes closed. Jose made her feel like there was a better life on the other side of the messed up things she'd been through.

"And all I want to do is love you and make you feel good." His lips were on her neck as she enjoyed the natural bliss between them.

After Sage's massage, they just held each other and talked about their future plans. "I want a lot of babies," Jose suddenly told her after she told him all about her dream wedding. Nobody would've ever thought, but deep down inside, she longed for a fairytale love story just like any other woman.

Chapter 12

"You are the most gorgeous woman I've ever seen," was how Jose greeted Sage when she woke up.

"And you're full of compliments. What are you up to?" She was smiling, but he was serious.

"I catch chills just looking at you. I'm gon' keep it real wit' you, Sage. I don't just want to be your boyfriend. I'm going to marry you one day." He kissed her hand as he gazed into her eyes lovingly.

Sage didn't know how to feel about that. It was flattering, but at the same time, it scared the shit out of her. "Is that right?" she asked nervously.

"It doesn't seem like that's in the plans for you." His eyes narrowed.

"I don't know what's in the plans for me... for us. I have to get used to this. Don't ruin it with the marriage talk, Jose."

"That scares you, huh?"

"It's not that…"

"Yes, it is." He chuckled. "I feel you. I'm just something for you to do."

"No, you ain't just something to do, but… marriage… that's a lifetime commitment. I ain't even twenty yet."

"My mom was eighteen when she married my pops." Jose's eyes were anxious.

"I'm not your mom."

When she said that he looked offended. "I don't mean that in a bad way," Sage added. "You said we were going to let this flow. Let it do just that, and I'm with you. If you rush me or try to push marriage on me, it's not going to result in a wedding. I can promise you that." Sage was already sick of the conversation.

"Okay, you're right, babe. I'm sorry." He kissed her hand. "I ain't trying to rush you, but the roles are reversed in this situation. I ain't used to begging for a woman's love. You got me messed up."

Sage already knew the reason for that. The average woman would make a man like him think she needed him. She had her own, and her independence at such a young age put her in a different situation. Not needing him for security or stability, Sage was indifferent about how far to take things with him.

"Speaking of other women. Do I have to worry about that?" She wanted to clarify that he wasn't dealing with drama that would interfere with her life. She'd had enough already.

"Not at all. I've been single for a while and since we started dealing, I ain't really been interested in nobody else."

"Okay, I'm going to see." Sage touched Jose's cheek before planting a kiss on her lips.

"You will." He kept right on kissing her until she giggled.

"I've really enjoyed spending quality time with you." Jose held her close to him.

"Me too." She melted in his embrace.

"How you feelin'?" He looked down at Sage with so much love evident in his eyes.

"I'm good, babe." She tried to assure him, but the pain in her leg was throbbing.

"You sure? It's like you're gritting your teeth or something." Being observant, Jose knew that something was wrong.

Putting his hand on her forehead, he noticed that she felt warm as hell. "It feels like you're running a fever."

"No, I'm fine." Sage was annoyed that he was fussing over her so much, although she did feel a little faint and weak.

"Are you sure? I was about to take you to grab some seafood at this spot not too far from here, but you may need to go to the hospital." He looked so worried that it made Sage feel bad.

"I'm okay. I'm just going to go take a quick shower, and we can go." When she stood up, her knees buckled.

Jose was right there by her side to break her fall. Picking her up, he gently placed her on the bed. "Oh shit, something's not right..." she whimpered as her eyes filled with tears.

"My leg, it really hurts." As her tears fell, he helped her get dressed and then carried her to his car.

Jose sped toward the highway and glanced over at Sage. The sheen of sweat shined on her face, and he also knew that something was really wrong. It was crazy because she'd seemed fine the night before and early that morning.

The drive from Lake Allatoona to Grady Medical was almost an hour, but Sage insisted that he take her there. She didn't want to deal with any new doctors, and although he understood, he wanted to take her somewhere closer. He pulled up near the ER's entrance and helped Sage out of the car. At that point, she still wasn't steady on her feet, so he carried her inside.

After explaining what was going on to the woman at the front desk, Jose watched as Sage was whisked away to the back in a wheelchair. "Can I go with her?" he asked frantically when she appeared to have passed out.

"Not unless you're a relative or her husband, and you'll have to show proof," the woman at the desk stated.

"Shit," Jose cussed as he paced the floor. His first instinct was to call Vintage, but he didn't have her number. Then he thought about Danielle. She had called his phone when Sage was in the accident. If he went through his call log, maybe he could find her number and call her.

An hour had passed by and Danielle and Vintage had joined Jose at the hospital. Everybody's nerves were bad as they waited for the doctor to come out. Vintage wrung her hands together nervously. Sitting down was hard to do, so she found herself restless.

"Relax, Vin, she's going to be okay," Danielle tried to assure her in a calm tone.

"I hope so Dani, but I'm just so worried. She was recovering so well. What could have possibly happened?" Vintage tried not to cry, but the tears slid down her cheeks anyway. Swiping them away, she was sick of crying. She convinced herself that from that moment on, she'd be stronger.

The same doctor who treated Sage after the car accident walked toward them. They were all relieved that they'd finally get some answers.

"Miss Saldana," he greeted her. "Your sister is in stable condition. It appears that she simply over-exerted herself." His eyes drifted to Jose as he grinned slyly. "You have to be very careful in making sure that she doesn't do anything too strenuous. She did just have major surgery reconstructing the bones in her thigh. As far as the fever, that's simply due to the fact that she's pregnant."

"Pregnant?" Vintage, Danielle and Jose asked in unison.

They were all shocked, especially Jose. His mouth was hanging open.

"Yes, she's at least a month along. You can go see her if you'd like. She's fine," the doctor added.

"Wow..." Jose whispered as a smile spread across his face. "She's pregnant."

Vintage wondered if the baby was his, but she would wait to ask her sister when they were alone. She quickly rose to her feet. "Uh, I think with this news, Jose should see her first alone."

Jose was on the doctor's heels anxious to talk to Sage about the good news. He hoped she didn't plan to get rid of it because the prospect of having a baby with her was something he looked forward too. That was not because he wanted to trap her, but because he really did love her. They had always used condoms until the night before, but maybe one of them had a microscopic hole in it or something. Then the thought of the baby being someone else's crossed his mind.

When he stepped in the room Sage was staring off into space. She seemed to be contemplating how she'd gotten pregnant just as Jose was. It was not something that either of them had planned. Then the reality that the baby may not be his smacked him in the face.

"Babe, how are you feeling?" Jose leaned over to kiss her forehead.

"I don't know." Her voice was monotone. "I take it that the doctor told you."

"Yeah, he did, but how do you feel about it?"

She sighed and sat up. Jose helped to adjust her pillows for her comfort. "I don't know about that either. In a way, I'm happy about it, but in a way, I wish it hadn't happened so early. It's yours too, so don't even question that. I've only been with you. How it happened? That's one thing I don't know. We always used condoms until the other night. Did the condom break, and you didn't tell me?"

"No, baby. I promise you that I wouldn't do no sneaky shit like that. If the condom had ever broken, you would've known right then. I don't play games like that. Shit happens baby. We never really slipped up but even condoms ain't one hundred percent," he told her.

"Yeah, but damn... I never thought for one second that I'd end up pregnant now. My period skipped a month, but I thought that was because I was taking so much medication. Then I thought it was stress. I haven't had one symptom of pregnancy, but I guess that's because it's so early."

"Are you going to keep it?" Jose's eyes were glued to hers. "Because I want you to."

"There's no way I'll abort our baby if that's what you're thinking, Jose. I don't know if I'm ready to be a mother, but I guess I have no say in the matter. This shit is happening either way," she stated firmly.

Jose kissed her hand. "I love you even more right now. I promise I'm going to be a father to our child whether we're together or not. I'd prefer we do it together though."

Tears shined in Sage's eyes. "I'd prefer we do it together too." Jose grabbed her hand and kissed her lips softly.

"So, there it is. We're in this together," he confirmed knowing that he would spend the rest of his life with her.

* * *

Sage had been released from the hospital the next day with strict instructions to take it easy. Because of her leg injury, she would have to be put on bed rest at the beginning of her third trimester. Sage wasn't feeling that at all, but she wanted to do everything in her power to assure that her baby was healthy.

"I'm ready to party one last time before this little munchkin takes over my body." Sage laughed as she rubbed her still flat belly.

Jose dropped down to his knees and kissed her belly. "I can't wait to meet him or her."

"Have you told your parents yet?" Sage questioned as he stood and kissed her lips.

"No. I'm waiting for you to meet them first." He stared down at her waiting for her to acknowledge that she wanted to meet them. He'd brought it up several times, but she never would respond.

"Okay, find out when it's a good time. I'm down." They shared a kiss and Jose held her tightly in his arms.

"Will do. So, are you ready to celebrate your birthday?" Jose asked still not letting her go.

"Yes, I am."

The small get together would be right there in the living room of the house she grew up in. She'd be surrounded by her closest friends and her sister. Her grandparents would be taking her out to dinner the next day. Jose grabbed her hand and led her to the celebration of her life.

Vintage had a knack for trying to make sure that everything was perfect. Jose had planned Sage's birthday celebration but asked for her assistance. She was happy to oblige, although she was shocked that her sister wanted something small and intimate. So far it was only about ten people there, but there was plenty of food and drinks for them to indulge in. They'd even hired a DJ.

The sound of the doorbell ringing made Vintage step away from things. There was hardly anyone there anyway, which was perfectly fine with her. Maybe more guests were arriving. She looked through the peephole and saw Stone standing there. She hadn't spoken to him since she told him she'd keep in touch.

"Damn," she whispered before opening the door. "Hi, Stone."

The look on his face was unreadable as she stared at the woman he longed for with all his being. She looked breathtaking in a sexy, short black cocktail dress. It was surely something a hot ass designer had created, but he didn't know which one. Vintage was all about labels even if you couldn't see them.

"Vintage," he said with a nod. "I was invited by Jose." Holding up a gift bag, he added. "This is for the birthday girl."

She stepped aside. "Well, come on in and give it to her yourself."

Stone shook his head. "What's up with you?" he asked as he stepped over the threshold.

"I've been busy with the real estate company since my boutique was burned down. I'm thinking of relocating to another building. The memories are too much. What's up with you?"

"I've been missing you and wondering why you can't make some time to even just talk to me. It's something between us, Vintage. You can try to make it go away all you want to, but it's not going anywhere. Not at all. Well, at least not on my end." Stone's stare was intense as he took in Vintage's essence. If only she wasn't so damn beautiful, he'd be able to let go. That wasn't just her outer beauty though. He knew that she was a good, loving person. Her passion for what she stood for was what had drawn him to her.

"I don't want you to think I don't care about you, Stone, I do. I'm just... well... to be completely one hundred about it, I don't trust you or any other man. It's hard to explain, but I'm afraid of what I feel for you. The fact is, I feel too much around you, and I felt it too soon. I think I'll lose my self-control with you and..."

Stone pulled her into his arms, letting her rest her head on his defined chest. "Don't you think it's about time that you let go for once. Love is about relinquishing that self-control. It's about experiencing what comes with the passion between us, and I don't mean that in a sexual way. Of course, I'd love to make love to you. It's all I think about at times. I'm still able to separate my physical attraction from my emotional ties to you. I want everything that comes with you, Vintage. Everything." He cupped her chin in his strong hand before crushing her lips with a kiss.

"Mmmm..." he moaned before pulling away. He didn't let her go.

"Shit, I missed you too, Stone." Vintage was finally able to admit it. "You know what. Fuck it. Let's do it. I want to be with you just as much as you want to be with me. I'm going to finally let go and allow my feelings to lead me, but if you do one thing to hurt or betray me, it's over. That simple."

"That simple," he repeated before kissing her again.

"So, you two are finally doing what comes naturally, huh?" Sage laughed ass he entered the room with Jose holding on to her arm.

Stone and Vintage separated and laughed.

"Happy birthday, Sage," Stone said with a smile as he passed her the gift bag he'd been holding on to.

"Thank you, brother-in-law." Sage flashed Vintage a look.

Vintage rolled her eyes thinking that her sister was taking things way too far like always.

"Thanks for coming man," Jose told Stone as they shared a pound.

"Thanks for inviting me," Stone confirmed.

"Well, let's go, baby. We have other guests to greet." Sage's eyes were still glued to Vintage's as she pulled Jose away. They left the lovebirds alone.

Vintage shook her head at her sister. She knew exactly what her eye contact meant. They could communicate silently. That was an uncanny gift they shared because they were so close. The message that Vintage got from Sage was that she and her Stone needed some time alone.

Vintage turned to look at Stone. "Why don't we go up to my room, to talk?" She grabbed a bottle of Patron and led him up the stairs before he could respond.

The look on Stone's face let her know that he was surprised at her sudden need for them to be alone with alcohol involved.

"You sure?" he confirmed with a sly look on his face.

"Shut up," she told him with a playful laugh. In Vintage's mind, life was too short, and she really did love Stone against her will. Whatever was meant to be would happen. Well, that was how she rationalized it anyway.

Once they were inside her bedroom, Vintage closed and locked the door. Her room was the size of a studio apartment and was decorated in the royal colors of purple and gold. The huge, king-sized canopy bed had purple and gold draping adoring the space. The purple comforter looked plush along with the multi-colored throw pillows that were propped against the headboard.

Pressing a button on the remote on the nightstand, Vintage smiled when the sound of old-school R&B flowed from the speakers. Lauryn Hill and D'Angelo were singing about how nothing even mattered other than their love. That was how Vintage was feeling at the moment about Stone, and she was tired of fighting it. He was like no other man she'd ever met in her life and for once, she was ready to take that plunge.

Before she sat down on the bed, she twisted the top off and drank the liquor straight from the bottle. Needing the liquid courage, she felt it burn its way down her esophagus. Stone grabbed the bottle, took it away from her and chuckled.

"Okay baby, what's going on?" His eyes were filled with sincerity as he asked.

"I have feelings for you, Stone," she admitted bashfully. "They came way too fast and I was... afraid. Fear is what makes me so... distant." She looked down at the floor. "I'm sorry for that. It's not you. It's me. You're a great guy. You're handsome, smart and caring. Shit, you're any woman's dream, but I'm just scared to lose you. I don't want to feel too much, and it's taken away from me. I'm so used to loss, and it's like I always expect it."

Stone put the bottle of liquor down on the nightstand. "You don't have to worry about that, Vintage. I'm not going anywhere. If you tell me you'll have me, that's it. I'm all in love. I really love you. Can't you see that." He caressed her face softly as he stared into her beautiful eyes.

Vintage didn't even hesitate to lean over and kiss him. The feeling of passion between them was undeniable and couldn't be extinguished. No matter how Vintage had tried, she couldn't resist him. It was like she had no control over herself like she once did. Stone had taken her will, and it had not been by force. She'd relinquished control when it came to a man for the first time in her adult life.

Was she ready to let it all go? He had won her heart fair and square, but was she ready to give him her body and soul? That was a hard one because the way he was kissing her and touching her was driving her insane. It was as if the need for him was making it hard for her to breath.

"Damn, mmm," she moaned into his mouth before he finally freed her lips.

"Damn is an understatement." His breathing was fast too as he pulled her into his arms.

His cologne was making it even harder to fight the way she felt. Going in for another kiss, she allowed her hands to wonder too. They pulled his shirt up and gently touched his pecs, then his abs. His body had to look amazing because his muscles were rock hard. When they parted again, she stared up into his eyes seeing pure longing.

Without speaking, he pushed her back on the bed. Vintage's breath caught because she had no idea what to do next. Should she tell him she wasn't ready? She didn't want to spoil the moment. Besides, she was the one who'd invited him up to her room. There was no turning back now, but was it too soon? There were all types of questions running through her mind.

"Just relax, baby. I won't do anything that you don't want me to do. It's just... I can't fight the urge to at least taste you. You don't have to do anything else." His voice was soothing and sweet, and Vintage felt so safe with him.

Her heart pounded hard enough for her to hear it. She'd never had a man perform oral sex on her before. Of course, Sage bragged about how incredible the feeling was. She'd explained to Vintage that it felt like your soul was leaving your body when it was good.

"If he knows what he's doing your whole world will be all messed up," Sage had laughed. "I'm telling you."

It was funny that her little sister was way more experienced sexually than she was. It defied all logic, and she was ready to feel what Sage had always boasted about. In Sage's opinion oral sex was better than penetration.

Vintage allowed Stone to pull her dress up over her head. After he removed her bra and thong, he stared down at her, shaking his head.

"Pure fucking perfection," he whispered allowing his warm hands to roam over her sexy body. "You are amazing, Vintage. What man in his right mind wouldn't want you, but you're mine now."

"All yours," she whispered as his hot, wet tongue traveled from her breasts down her torso.

The heat from his mouth was making her so damn hot with intense physical attraction. Vintage had never experienced an orgasm in her twenty-two years. Not even masturbating, she wasn't prepared for what was happening to her.

"Ohhh... shit... Stone... what... what... the hell are you doing?" Her eyes were wide.

Stone didn't say a word as he continued with his tongue's assault. Like an expert, he had her legs shaking as she ground into his tongue. "Making you cum," he said as he looked up at her.

"My goodness..." she gasped. The feeling was better than she'd ever expected. It made her want to take things to the next level. Would she let him penetrate her? Was she ready for that because she was nowhere near ready for what he was doing to her now?

Suddenly, she knew what her sister meant because it really felt like her heart stopped and her soul had left her body. What the fuck? It was hard for her to catch her breath. It was crazy because as her leg shook, she couldn't control her body's spasms. Stone just kept right on sucking on her hardened clit, and as multiple orgasms ripped through her body, she didn't know how to handle it. Her nerves were on overdrive.

"You taste so good," Stone said as he drank from her fountain of love.

Vintage wanted to return the favor, but she didn't know how. Not only that, but she had never felt such overwhelming pleasure before.

"Wow. That felt... amazing." She held onto him for dear life.

"I'm glad it did because that's only the beginning of where I can take your body." He held her close to him. "We should get back to your sister's party. We got plenty of time to spend together since you're mine now."

"All yours," Vintage confirmed as they kissed.

She went into the bathroom to freshen up before putting her clothes back on. Stone held her in his arms before leading her back downstairs. "I love you, Vintage."

"And I love you too, Stone." Vintage winked at him as they joined the intimate celebration of her sister's life. She'd defied the odds more than once, and Vintage was just grateful that she still had her sister in her life.

There weren't many people there and Sage wanted it that way. At first, it had surprised Vintage, but she knew that her sister was in a different place now. Not only did she have another chance at life, but she was pregnant. Life was full of surprises, and sometimes they were actually good ones.

Everybody sang happy birthday to Sage and Vintage realized that in a few short months they'd also be planning a baby shower. Shit, the way she and Jose were acting, they'd be planning a wedding. The thought made Vintage smile. She never thought in a million years that her sister would fall in love and have a family. The revelation made her cry. Sage had come full circle and who would have ever imagined that? If anything, everybody would've thought Vintage would've been married with children first.

Sage looked so happy and content as her face glowed. Vintage realized that her sister had grown up in such a short time right before her eyes. It was crazy that it took such dire measures for her to see life in a different light, but at least it had happened. Instead of being envious of her sister's happiness, Vintage was pleased.

Chapter 13

The next two months flew by and Vintage was experiencing a whirlwind romance with Stone. They'd been on a Caribbean cruise and visited the island of Maldives. Among them were Amsterdam and Greece. Stone didn't resist to spoil his woman. She was his indeed, and all they both wanted to do was finally bond physically as a couple. Vintage felt like she was ready, but Stone didn't want her to think he was rushing her.

"Babe, you don't have to do anything you don't want to do," he assured her over the phone.

Vintage was rubbing coconut oil on her body after her shower. "Whatever I do, believe me, I want to do it."

"Okay, you're a grown woman. You know what you're doing."

Exactly."

"Once we go there, it ain't no turning back," Stone told her in a joking voice.

"Boy bye." Vintage laughed. "I'm ready. I love you."

"And I love you more."

"You promise?"

"On my life."

Vintage giggled. "Be careful about that now, baby."

"I'm so careful. I'm so in love with you, and you know it."

"I do," she admitted because she could really feel how much Stone loved her.

It was crazy that she may be losing her virginity that night right there in Atlanta instead of overseas. The thought made her giggle. They'd been to so many romantic places, and she was able to hold out. Now, she felt the need to go all the way with him. She was finally ready to let go and let love take over.

Stone had planned a romantic night for them to hit the town and Vintage was excited. When she saw the black, stretch Hummer a smile creased her face. "What is this?

"I decided we're going to go all out tonight, so I got a driver."

"Okay, baby... You get a point tonight. Since you ain't driving, we can actually make out and stuff." Vintage laughed.

"Woman stop teasin' me, damnit!" Stone grabbed her and pulled her close to his side.

"I'm not," Vintage told him in an innocent voice. "I'm down for whatever."

Stone grabbed her hand and kissed it. "I'm not trying to rush you. We got time, and I'm patient enough to wait for you."

All the teasing was starting to get to Vintage. She wanted to experience more with Stone. He just did things to her that no other man before him had done.

"Baby, I won't do anything I don't want to do, so when I do something, don't stop me. Okay," she told him sternly.

"Okay," he confirmed, taken aback by her directness.

He knew that she meant, *in other words, if I give you the pussy tonight, you better 11111111111111111111111111take it.* They got in the back of the stretch Hummer and just as Vintage had said, they were able to share wet kisses. He couldn't keep his hands off her. Their first stop was for dinner at Chops Steak House.

"You know you're wrong for looking as good as you do," Stone complimented Vintage before kissing her neck softly.

They went inside the restaurant and the patrons looked on as though they were a famous couple. They seemed to exude an aura of prestige and wealth. Well put together, they were aiming to be the power couple that everyone made them out to be.

After a delectable dinner of filet mignon, baked potatoes and grilled asparagus, they headed to their next destination. Unable to keep their hands to themselves, they were just as lovey-dovey when they arrived at a club in Buckhead called Tongue and Groove. Vintage wasn't surprised that it was salsa night.

After showing her moves off and sweating on the dance floor without a care, she and the love of her life headed to his place. She'd been there a few times. It was a nice one-bedroom condo on the sixth floor of a building on Piedmont Rd. The view was magnificent, and she loved the aura and hustle and bustle of the city life.

Once they crossed his home's threshold, she kicked her heels off and went out on the balcony. He walked up behind her and wrapped his arms around her waist before inhaling the scent of her skin. "You have some type of spell on me. I'm convinced." He shook his head as he felt defeated.

"No, you love me, that's all." She smiled and touched his arm. "Love isn't a spell at all. It's that real shit."

"Damn right it is." Stone's grip was tighter around her waist as he pulled her into him.

The next thing Vintage knew Stone had picked her up, and she wrapped her legs around his waist. Feeling

232

that heat between them take over her, she was not willing to change her mind. She was ready to give the most intimate part of herself to him.

As he placed her gently on the bed, they engaged in a passionate kiss. Their tongues wrestled, and Vintage indulged in the sweet bliss. The heat of his tongue on her collarbone made her shiver. "Mmm..." she moaned as her body shuddered.

Stone's hands were all over her. "Are you sure you want to..."

Vintage ended his words with another kiss. That was when Stone started to remove her clothes. His hands cupped her thick ass cheeks as he let out a guttural grunt. He wanted her so bad that it was animalistic. Staring deeply into his eyes, Vintage wondered why she was so willing to lose her virginity to him and not a man from her past. They hadn't even been together for a year yet, but it was just something about him.

Soon, he was slurping hungrily on her aroused clitoris. As she writhed and moved beneath him, he held her in place before placing his middle finger inside of her wet, tightness. Her muscles tightly clenched the powerful orgasm caused her body to tremble.

"Ohhhh... my... Stone..." A lone tear fell from her eyes.

Moving up her torso, Stone's lips touched her allowing Vintage to taste herself. She'd become familiar with her flavor since he didn't hesitate to taste her all the time. Now, she was ready to take things to another level. She wanted to learn how to please him.

Looking down at her exquisite beauty, Stone was tempted to ask her one more is she was sure, but he could tell by the look in her eyes that she was. He leaned over to retrieve a condom from the nightstand. Grabbing the condom from his hand, she ripped it open. After removing the rubber from the wrapper, she clutched his hardness with her soft hand slid the condom down his shaft before leading him inside of her wetness.

The feeling took Stone's breath away. Holding on to her, he closed his eyes trying to be gentle, but the heat

234

from her depths along with the tightness made him want to go so deep. Damn, she was extremely wet. The sounds were driving him crazy because it sounded like he'd plunged into an ocean.

"You okay, baby?" he asked, gazing into her eye. He noticed that she was flinching, and she was making it hard for him to fill her with his length.

"Yes," she whispered.

"Relax and open up for me," he coaxed as he kissed her neck. "I don't want to hurt you."

"I know..."

Stone held on to her hips and ground slowly in a circle until she finally loosened up for him. "Arrgghh...yeah... damn Vintage."

"Mmm..." Vintage started to match the rhythm of his thrusts and the pain subsided into pleasure.

Stone had already placed a towel under her because they both know that she would bleed. He didn't even feel any diversion toward something so natural. He was the first man to explore her sugary walls, and he would always relish in that.

"Mmm... you feel so fuckin' good..." he growled as he guided her hips with his strong hands. "You okay baby?" Dipping down, Stone softly sucked on her bottom lip.

"Yesss... ohhh... Stone... what the... what are you doing to me?" To Vintage it felt as if he was pushing against some kind of pleasure button or something.

It was causing a deep warm sensation to settle in the pit of her stomach and it was spreading. The tingles were starting to become even more intense.

"I'm making love to you..." His voice was breathless. "Mmm... your pussy's so tight."

Stone bit down on his bottom lip as Vintage ran her fingernails along his back. Her eyes closed as he stimulated her G-Spot to no end. Vintage knew how a clitoral orgasm felt, but that was something different. Her body rocked against Stone's as she creamed all over his hardness.

"Ohhhh..." he stared down at her and shook his head. "Shit, I could live inside you..."

His grip on her waist was tight as he rode his own orgasm out. The way his body convulsed and shook on top of her, Vintage wondered if he was okay. When he smiled and slapped her gently on the ass, she knew that she'd pleased him. The thought made her smile too.

"Wow, that was amazing." Vintage felt Stone get soft inside of her.

"Shit..." He was out of breath. "I'm sorry, babe. I didn't think I'd have a pull-out game when it comes to you. Damn."

She was on birth control, but the condom was an extra incentive. She'd given herself to him, but she wasn't ready to be a mother yet. Sometimes she was bad about taking her pills, so a condom would always be an incentive. It was a good thing they'd talk all the proper precautions because she didn't want to spoil their moment with worries of being pregnant.

* * *

The next few months flew by and Vintage was feeling like she'd finally found the man for her. Sage and Jose had even gotten engaged a month earlier. The gender reveal for their baby was scheduled along with the baby shower in a few weeks and Vintage was looking forward to knowing whether she'd be having a niece or nephew. Not that it mattered to her, but gender reveals were the big thing lately.

She'd just pulled up to Stone's two-story Victorian style house in Fayetteville, Ga. It was furnished beautifully and modern, but there was still that warmth that made her feel like she was at home. He'd offered to cook for her for the first time, and she was excited.

Before she could even ring the doorbell, Stone swung the door open. He greeted her with a sweet kiss before inviting her in. The aroma of something delicious cooking teased her senses, making her mouth water.

"Wow, something smells good."

"Well, you know. I can burn."

"You're always bragging, so I know this food better be better than anything I've ever tasted,"

Stone chuckled and took Vintage's black P-Coat. After hanging it on the coat rack near the door, he admired her delicious body in a cream colored jumpsuit. Her black knee-high boots were high and made her seem way taller than he was used to. He still towered over her though.

"I don't know about it tasting better than anything you've had, but I assure you it'll taste good."

"So, are going to tell me what you're cooking."

"No." He kissed her softly on the tip of her nose. "It's a surprise. It'll be done in about twenty minutes, so make yourself at home. Kick off your shoes and watch some TV. I'll bring you a glass of wine."

"Okay, will do." She actually did take her boots off and lounged on the sofa with the remote in her hand. Soon he bought her a glass of Chardonnay.

"Hmm... now I can get used to this." He smiled at her before walking off to the kitchen.

Hearing him say that made Vintage's smile grow even wider. She didn't want to jump the gun, but something told her that she'd met her husband. After they made love for the first time, it sent their relationship to another plateau. It was as if they'd both fallen even deeper in love, and the passion was only getting stronger. She sipped on her wine as she mused.

Before Vintage could get deep into another episode of *Forensic Files,* Stone entered the room. "You do like watching that kind of shit. See, now I'm scared of your ass."

Vintage flashed a frown his way. "What are you trying to say, scary ass?"

"That women who watch that type of shit are crazy as hell. Y'all be plotting on how to get away with murder."

They both laughed.

"Don't give me a reason to use what I know then." She narrowed her eyes at him.

Pretending that he was shaking out of fear, Stone dramatically fell into the wall with his hands out. "Don't, don't kill me, baby..."

"You're such an actor. Is the food ready? My stomach keeps on growling. You told me not to eat before I got here, so..."

"I'm sorry, baby girl, dang. Calm down. You gon' hurt me 'cause I ain't cooking fast enough? The hell?" he asked playfully. "Nah, for real. I was coming to let you know the food is ready, so you can come to eat, with your beautiful self."

"Thank you, sweetness," she said all innocent like she wasn't just going off because she was hungry.

"Don't even try it. You was just 'bout to take my head off. Don't be my friend now 'cause you 'bout to eat."

"Shut up, boy," she shot at him playfully before following him into the kitchen.

"Boy? Where you see a lil' boy at?" He looked around. "All man right here, and you know it. You've felt it."

241

"A big dick does not make you a man," she teased as she sat down at the table.

"Your mouth is real smart tonight, Miss Lady. I'm gon' have to tame you." The sly grin on his face let her know what that meant.

"Tame me? Hmm... you might be the one getting tamed."

"Now, that shit just turned me the fuck on."

"So, what did you cook? Can you reveal the big surprise now?" Vintage was a picky eater and she didn't want to hurt his feelings if he'd cooked something she didn't like.

"You remember that recipe you posted on your Facebook page? You said you wanted to try to cook it yourself, but you never did."

"Uh huh, the garlic honey salmon. Oh my god, it looked so good. Is that what you cooked?" Her mouth was really watering as she hoped that he had cooked that shit right.

"Yup and I tasted it. It's so delicious."

"What did you make with it?"

"Mashed potatoes and stir-fried vegetables. It's some zucchini, squash, broccoli and cauliflower. I'm having you for dessert though since you lookin' all sweet. You can have some cheesecake."

"You're a mess." Vintage grinned slyly as he fixed her plate and placed it in front of her. Then he prepared his food and sat down at the table.

They blessed their food and dug in. "Mmm, this is good." Vintage couldn't help but enjoy the way the flavors danced on her tongue. "You did that baby."

"Hmm, it's some other things I wanna do." He flashed her a serious look that made her want to put her fork down and jump on his ass.

Playing it cool, she ignored his sexual advances as hard as it was. "Uh, I'm tryin' to eat right now."

"Me too." The desire that burned in his eyes told her that he didn't give one damn about eating any food.

"I don't think you're referring to the food," she pointed out.

"Nope, but I'll let you eat. Soon as that plate's clean, I'm eating that pussy right here on this table." His eyes moved from her to the table and back again for emphasis.

Vintage started eating fast as hell, and Stone couldn't help but laugh. "Don't choke babe. I ain't goin' nowhere."

Vintage never thought something could feel so good in her life, but the way he ate her out was like nothing she'd ever experienced before. It felt so good that she couldn't help but think that what Sage had told was an understatement.

Soon the table was cleared, and Stone had Vintage laid out on the table spread eagle.

"Ohhhh... myyyy..." Her pupils rolled back as she held on to the back of Stone's head.

The orgasmic ride that he was taking her on was nothing compared to when he took her upstairs to his bedroom. That time, Vintage didn't care that he didn't bother to put on a condom. It was the first time they'd slipped up, but it probably wouldn't be the last.

* * *

Of course, Vintage had ended up spending the night. She had before, so Stone had designated a couple of drawers for her things. Therefore, she had underwear and a change of clothes for the next day.

"Don't leave before I get off work. I want to see your face when I get home. Shit, I'd love to see your pretty ass face every day when I get home." His gorgeous eyes sparkled with love.

"But babe, I have some things to handle today," she protested.

He caressed her face. "Can you do it tomorrow, please. Just be here when I get back. Okay?"

With a nod, she finally relented before they shared a sweet kiss. As she stood at the door and watched him leave, she had a blanket wrapped around her naked body. After she closed the door, she rushed upstairs to take a shower.

Drunk off love, she staggered to the master bath, knocking a bamboo jewelry box onto the floor. A gold

Rolex watch slid out and sparked a memory in Vintage's mind. It looked just like her one of her father's watches that had been taken the night of her parents' murders.

Her heartbeat quickened as she turned the watch over to see if there was an inscription.

Never forget that you are my love. 9/25

Vintage dropped the watch on the carpeted floor after she read the words out loud. That was exactly what was engraved on her father's watch. Her mother had given it to him on their tenth anniversary. They'd been married on September 25th.

Vintage picked up her cell phone with her fingers trembling. Why would Stone have the Rolex that her mother had given her father? There was no way that shit was a coincidence. She found Stone's name in her contacts and dialed his number.

"Hello, everything okay, babe?"

"No, so you need to find some excuse for you to leave work and get here, now!"

Chapter 14

Stone's nervous eyes told Vintage that something was terribly wrong when she held the watch up and screamed at him.

"Where the fuck did you get this?" Her voice was frantic because she needed answers. No matter how she tried to rationalize it in her mind, it just didn't make any sense.

"Sit down, babe. We need to talk." He was all calm about it, but she could sense his apprehension.

"Oh, yes we do because this shit right here isn't making any sense to me." She was still holding the watch up in the air.

As she sat down on the sofa, Stone took in a deep breath before he revealed everything to her. His mind drifted to the last time he'd seen his own father.

* * *

Two months earlier

"Pops, I'm out. I can't do it," Stone told his father without being able to look at him.

When Stone's father asked him to find Vintage and Sage about four months earlier, he didn't think he'd feel the way he did about Vintage. His father had asked him to do something that he'd never thought of doing. Being a professional, white collar type, he wasn't the one to do illegal shit. His father was though. He'd been locked up for fraud, and it wasn't just any kind of fraud. He was a stockbroker who had taken millions from unsuspecting victims in a Ponzi scheme. The entire time he took other people's investments with the promise of them turning a profit when he knew that they wouldn't. When his trial ended, he was given the maximum of fifteen years in prison. He could've taken a plea deal for five, but he refused.

"The fuck you mean, you're out?" Stone's father looked around at the guards to see if they were paying attention. "They owe me and you. You know that. I've been telling you that for years."

Stone had just found his father, Rocc Phillips, about five years ago. After his mother passed away from lung cancer a year before, she finally revealed who his estranged father was, and the fact that he was incarcerated.

Stone had never known who he was. His mother also confessed that she met him when she was the receptionist for MS Realty. His father was a private investor who had invested over a half million dollar in the business. Mendosa had promised that Rocc's investment would quadruple in the next few years. Once Rocc was behind bars, he never saw a dime of that money. As much as he had asked Mendosa to give him his investment for a good lawyer, he didn't.

A few months before that he'd visited his father and he told him, "Mendosa promised that if anything happened to me, you would at least be taken care of. He may not have paid for my counsel, but he owed me." Stone's father then told him that a key would be mailed to him in a few days. "It goes to a safe deposit box. I want you to get everything that's in it. When I didn't get what I was owed, I sent some of my... men to... handle it. All they got was some jewelry and a safe with a hundred thousand dollars in it. That's not nearly what Mendosa owed me. I want you to get the money from that safe deposit box. Use it to do what you have to do to get what we are both owed. I don't care what you have to do. Kill the bitches if that's a must."

"Pops, I ain't no killer." Stone was terrified about what his father was asking of him. Part of him felt like he just had to do it though. He'd always wanted his father's love and acceptance and doing his bidding was probably the only way to get it. Stone just promised himself that he wouldn't kill for it.

The next day he went to the bank to retrieve the items in the safe deposit box. There was the watch that Vintage had found and twenty-five thousand dollars in cash. Knowing that he wasn't down for it, Stone only agreed when he did his research and saw how beautiful Vintage was. He'd fallen in love at first sight and knew then that he would never do anything to hurt her. It just took him a while to tell his father that.

"She's not the blame for what her father did, and I can't carry the blame for what you asked me to do either. I'm going to tell her the truth," Stone confessed.

"What? You want me to get time for murder?" Rocc asked him through clenched teeth.

"You did get her parents killed. Maybe you deserve time for murder. Either way, I'm not going to hurt her or steal her money. It's not going to happen. I love her."

"You pussy whipped son of a bitch!" Rocc stood up and pounded on the table before lunging toward his son. "You've ruined every fucking thing!"

The correctional officers rushed over and restrained him as Stone backed up. He knew that there was no turning back.

*   *   *

Vintage deserved some closure about her parents' deaths, but unless she found that watch, Stone was going to keep it to himself. Now that she'd found that bit of evidence, he had to tell the truth. There was no way that he was going to prison for something he didn't do.

"I'm so sorry, Vin. I never had any intentions on hurting you. None. I fell for you and..."

Vintage stood up with a smirk on her face. "So, you mean to tell me that your father had my parents killed over money. Then he asked you to get what he felt was rightfully his, and you agreed to it even if it meant that you had to kill me and my sister?"

"I never agreed to that." Stone was at a loss for words, but he knew that he had to do something. He had never seen that look in Vintage's eyes before. "I love you."

"You don't love shit, Stone! You should have told me this from the beginning, but no! You were going to keep this shit to yourself! What then? What if your father hired somebody else to take me and my sister out? Huh?" Tears slid from her eyes. "Fuck you, Stone! I should've known better! You ain't shit just like every other man I've been with! Actually, you're worse. You know what the fuck I was going through. You used my vulnerability against me! All this time, you've just been using me for some money that my father owes yours! It's no excuse for that shit, you, asshole! I fuckin' hate your ass!" As she sobbed, she grabbed her purse and headed toward the door. "I never want to hear from you or see you again! I'm going to let the police know that your fuckin' father killed my parents! You can't stop me because me and my sister need justice! Would you have really killed me, Stone?" Her eyes softened as she asked.

"No! Hell no! I told my father that I would hack into your bank account and transfer the money into an account that he had overseas. I never had any intentions of doing anything to you or Sage. I just knew that I had to meet you." As Stone, closed the space between them, Vintage backed up and grabbed the doorknob.

"Get the fuck away from me!" she screamed when he tried to touch her.

"I'm so sorry I didn't tell you the truth from the beginning, baby. I'm in love with you, and I'll never let anybody hurt you. I swear." Stone's face and tone seemed sincere, but Vintage wasn't buying it.

"If you really gave a shit about me, you would've told me all this a long time ago! Since you didn't, I don't want to have anything else to do with you! Nothing, Stone! Is that even your real fuckin' name? Are you really an accountant? What else have you not been telling me?"

"Yes, my name is Stone and I am an accountant. Everything else I've told you is true."

"Well, that's no incentive. I wish I'd never met you! Don't contact me again. Forget me, Stone. Forget you ever met me, you lying ass piece of shit!" With that said, she opened the door and stormed toward her car.

Stone followed her, pleading his case and the love that he felt. Vintage wasn't trying to hear it though. She was done with him, and her first stop, when she left his house, would be the Fulton County Police Department. Tears blinded her view, but she wiped them away. She knew that she would never be able to be with Stone after that. At first, she thought he would be her husband, but now she knew that he was only sent to her to reveal what

had really happened to her parents. At least she had

some closure about that. It was no consolation though.

Her heart was broken, and she knew that she'd never

love again.

Epilogue

Over a year had passed and Stone's father had been sentenced to life in prison. Stone had reluctantly given up the watch for evidence, although he didn't want to be the one to throw his own father under the bus. His love for Vintage had just been that damn strong.

To his surprise, his father had sent him a letter promising that he wouldn't pursue the issue with the Saldana sisters any longer. They weren't the blame for their father's promise to him, and Stone hoped that he had finally come to grips with that.

Vintage had not been joking when she said that she didn't want to see or talk to him anymore. Over time, he gave up... but not completely. She'd opened another boutique not that far from the other one. Of course, Stone had looked her up on the internet.

When he saw Vintage's new candy apple red, BMW convertible, his heart caught in his throat. For some reason, she didn't have the top down that time. He'd seen her a few times before and only watched. Not man enough to approach her, he stayed in his car.

That day, he watched as she got out of her car and walked over to the backseat with a huge smile on her face. As she opened the door, he noticed that she was getting something out of the backseat. When he saw her holding a baby boy who was about four months old, Stone's heart sank. It sank even further when he saw a man get out of the passenger seat. Dude took the little boy from her and walked inside of the boutique.

Stone couldn't help but do the math and wondered if the baby boy was his. His vision was good, and his eyes had zoomed right in on him. That little boy looked more like him than that nigga she was with. Then he remembered who he was. It was the same dude who had posted that video of Vintage's breasts. She had ended up with the same man that he had comforted her about.

As Stone hit the gas and sped off, he realized that he'd made the biggest mistake in his life. He would never force Vintage to let her be in their son's life, but he knew that little boy was his. He felt it in his heart. It was as if his life was repeating history. His father hadn't been there for him, and now he wouldn't be able to be there for his own son. Karma was definitely a bitch.

KS Oliver

ORDER FORM
DIAMANTE' PUBLICATIONS, LLC
2483 Heritage Village 16-341
Snellville, GA 30078

Name (please print):_____

Address:_____

City/State:_____

Zip:_____

QTY	TITLES	PRICE

KS Oliver

DO YOU HAVE A LOVED ONE ON LOCK ???

Diamante PUBLICATIONS

Dear Supporter,

I'm sure that we can all agree on one thing: literacy is an important skill that everyone should be allowed to exercise. Whether you're a lover of gritty street drama, erotic enlightenment, or riveting romance, the opportunity to avail yourself of quality reads to sharpen your mind and sate your thirst for literature should always be available to you no matter who you are or where you are.

Diamante' Publications believes in equal opportunity where literacy is concerned. In line with our beliefs, we've developed Diamonds on Lock, a prison book program that provides incarcerated readers with quality reading material monthly at a cheaper rate. By enrolling your imprisoned loved one in this program you are not only supporting literacy but also showing your family member/friend that you love them and you support their interests.

How Does It Work?

Book Selection: Subscribed inmates will receive three (3) Diamante' Publications novels monthly. As your inmate's D.O.L. subscriber, you must visit the Diamonds on Lock webpage monthly to select your inmate's book choices or three (3) novels will be randomly selected by our staff.

Payments: Monthly subscriptions are $25.00 per inmate. Subscription payments must be made online solely via the D.O. L. (Diamante' Publications) website. Subscriptions are pay as you go with no contract holding you to monthly obligations. For each month that you desire for your inmate to receive a shipment, you simply pay the subscription fee for that month. For your inconvenience, you have the choice of also paying for multiple months upfront to ensure that your inmate receives a shipment for each of those months. Book selections will only be sent out upon receipt of payment.

Shipment: Each month your inmate's book selections will be sent directly to them from us. Simply provide us with their complete institution mailing address and inmate number to assure proper delivery.

It's really just that easy. With the click of a button and for only $25.00 per month at your discretion, you can put hot and new releases in the palms of your loved ones hands. We at Diamante' Publications thank you for your interest in maintaining active literacy skills and going above and beyond to support your inmate's reading interests. We look forward to serving you and building a lasting relationship that will enhance the overall literary community.

Sincerely,
Ebonee' Oliver, CEO
Brandon Abby, President

KS Oliver

Stay tuned as Diamante' Publications has
plenty more heat for you

Join our mailing list
diamantepublications@gmail.com

To see what's releasing next, read a sneak peek
or win great prizes

YOU CAN ALSO VISIT US AT
www.diamantepublications.com

Please leave us on a Review
@Amazon.com
@Goodreads.com

Let's Connect
Facebook @AuthoressKS
Instagram @AuthoressKS
Twitter @AuthoressKS

Made in the USA
Columbia, SC
07 July 2019